Keatyn's Journey

Leah Brewer

Copyright © 2022 Leah Brewer

Third Edition 2024

The characters and events portrayed in this book are fictitious. Any similarity to real persons, living or dead, is coincidental and not intended by the author.

All rights reserved. No part of this book may be reproduced, stored in a retrieval system, or transmitted in any form or by any means, electronic, mechanical, photocopying, recording, or otherwise, without the express permission of the author.

ISBN-13: 979-8-9864921-0-0

Cover design by Leah Brewer; Front Cover Image photo by Shelby Biggers from SMB Photography.

Scripture is taken from the New King James Version®. Copyright © 1982 by Thomas Nelson. Used by permission. All rights reserved.

In memory of Keatyn Rebecca Snead, beautiful baby girl loved and missed by so many since 2005.

Author's Note

Nearly three years ago, I set out on a deeply personal mission to bring Keatyn's Journey to life. Since its release, I have had to navigate the painful reality of losing my beloved cover model, Samantha—a radiant spirit whose light shone brightly and whose presence brought joy to all around her.

I cherished her deeply, and her absence is felt profoundly every day by all who loved her. In her honor, I made the decision to revisit and revise the book, aiming to elevate it so that it is something both Keatyn and Samantha would be proud to represent.

Thank you to everyone who took the time to read and review Keatyn's Journey. Your insightful comments were invaluable in shaping this revision. May God bless you all!

Chapter 1

After years of heartache, Keatyn Griffin finally accepted that God had abandoned her. What use could He possibly have for someone like her?

Her chest constricted as she stared, unseeing, out the window, her mind on the last sermon she'd heard years earlier. The preacher's words about God's love had burned into her mind and stayed there. Maybe because it had been the last time her family had gathered together. The last time she'd been able to breathe without a weight trying to suffocate her.

Memories of the night that changed her life threatened to overtake Keatyn as her hand trailed over the puckered scar on her left arm. Like an anchor, the weight of her past always seemed to keep her from moving forward. Peter Brockton, her boyfriend, had been hinting at marriage for the past few months. What if she married him, and the first time he had the chance, he left her to die? Could she trust a man to take care of her?

She shook off the memory as she stepped up to the mirror. Swallowing tears, she gazed at her reflection. The face staring back at her was not the same one that had moved to Seattle many years prior. Then, the person looking back at her was joyful, full of mischief, and happy. It had been the face of a carefree eighteen-year-old ready to take on the world.

The person in the mirror was now a bitter twenty-six-year-old. Full of hurt. Of sadness. Maybe even hatred. This face was blotchy red and way too white for her liking. She missed the beach. The feeling of sand between her toes as the sun beat down her face. She missed Pensacola Beach. But she would never see it again.

A stack of mail stared at her from the coffee table. Usually, that wouldn't bother her. But the letter on top couldn't have been less desirable if it had been from the Internal Revenue Service.

It was from Myles Griffin. The man who used to be her father.

She'd been dodging his calls for the past few months. It was better that way. She had no use for him after everything that happened. She'd tried to give him subtle hints over the past ten years, but that hadn't worked.

She grudgingly admitted that a tiny part of her wanted to see him again. Her heart hammered like a battlefield of conflicting emotions, torn between the need for closure and the desire to keep her distance.

Keatyn glanced at Mama's Bible sitting on the bookcase. Guilt spread through her body, but she pushed it aside. Surely, Mama wouldn't expect her to stay in contact with the man who left her to die. So, why should she?

Because Mama was a loving, forgiving woman. The burden of forgiveness felt heavier than the scar on Keatyn's arm.

She ripped open the envelope and took a deep breath before allowing her eyes to focus on the page.

Dear Keatyn,

For some reason, you continue to push me away. I've racked my brain looking for a way to get you back — but that's hard when you won't even talk to me.

Do you blame me for your mama's death? I would say so since I blame myself. How can I express my utter despair? My sorrow? What can I do to make you understand? I'll do whatever it takes.

I would gladly trade my life for your mama's. But that's not how things work.

I won't see her again in this life, but I take comfort knowing I will see her in the next. My prayer is that you'll also see her but that's up to you. Please don't let bitterness and anger keep you from seeing her again. I beg you.

We're having a birthday party for Alvin soon. He wants so badly to celebrate your birthdays together. Please come. For him.
I love you—more than you'll ever know. And I'll never stop trying to gain your forgiveness.

Love always,
Dad

Her birthday was a couple of weeks before Alvin's. When they were kids, they would sometimes celebrate together. But it had been years.

Sobs racked her body as she wadded up the paper. Why had God abandoned her?

Why?

Chapter 2

Keatyn sighed and closed her laptop. She swirled around in her office chair and glanced at Lucy Parnell. "Lucy, have you heard that Chad plans to announce his retirement at the end of the year?"

Keatyn crossed her legs and grinned. With her designer jeans and a navy-blue silk button-up top, she had no doubt she gave off a casual chic vibe. Her Louis Vuitton booties rounded out the look and screamed money.

Even though Lucy had recently turned twenty-nine, she could pass for a schoolgirl in her green plaid skirt and cream sweater. She spun around in her chair and met Keatyn's gaze. "Girl, yes. Are you planning on putting your name in the hat for his replacement?"

"Oh, a hundred percent." Keatyn narrowed her eyes and pinned Lucy with her gaze. "Are you?"

Lucy lowered her voice. "No, I'm not even remotely ready for that role. I have my eye on that Director spot. Just waiting for Derek to transfer out."

Matching Lucy's calm tone, Keatyn scooted closer to Lucy. "Is he planning on transferring?"

Lucy glanced around before scooting her chair right next to Keatyn's. "He recently reconnected with his high school sweetheart. So, he wants to move back to West Virginia. He's interviewing at one of the branches there next week."

"Nice." Keatyn leaned forward, propping her elbows on the desk. "Keep me posted."

"I will." Lucy took a sip of her coffee. "Hey, do you have plans for the fourth?"

"Peter asked me to go to his parents." Keatyn rolled her eyes. "They're having a party."

"I can't believe you." Lucy clucked her tongue. "That man is a big-time catch. And you treat him like he's a nuisance."

Keatyn yawned before turning to log out of her computer. "I do not. I don't care for his mother. That's all."

Lucy giggled and shook her head. "She's pretty awesome if you ask me."

A smirk crossed Keatyn's face as she propelled herself out of the chair. "It's a good thing I didn't ask you."

⚓

A few days later, Keatyn brewed a cup of white chocolate mocha and settled onto her mauve velvet sofa. Her loft-style apartment matched her lifestyle perfectly. Upon entering the front door, a breathtaking view of the lake overlooked an open and airy living area. While the view of the lake wasn't exactly a beach, it was still a beautiful sight.

She opened a self-help book on managing employees and started reading a chapter about coaching.

Her cell phone buzzed. Her spine stiffened as Myles Griffin's name flashed across the screen. She'd changed it from Dad a few years ago. It seemed more fitting to call him by his proper name now.

She'd never understand why he continued calling her. Maybe he needed to hear how she felt about talking to him. Again.

Keatyn held up a slim finger before pressing the green button. "Yes, Myles." She sighed loudly, hoping he'd get the point.

There was a brief pause before he greeted her with his happy voice. "Happy Birthday, Keatyn."

"Why do you continue to call me on my birthday?"

He cleared his throat, and his voice became less upbeat this time. Good. "Because you're my daughter, and I love you."

"That's your problem, not mine."

"Please give me a chance. Come home."

"I've told you a million times that I will not be coming back to that place."

"Your family wants to see you, Keatyn. We miss you. We love you."

"I'm at the only home I have. Washington. And you all ceased to be my family the day you let Mama die in that fire."

"Keatyn, please–"

"No. The only thing I need from you is for you to lose my number."

She hit the end button and slung her phone across the room. It hit the wall with a thump before cracking onto the tile floor. Ignoring the phone, she bolted off the sofa and marched onto the balcony. Maybe that'll be the last time he calls.

After a few minutes, she walked inside and picked up the book. Her mind kept going back to that night. She slammed the book shut and placed it on the bookcase. As she turned to walk away, Mama's Bible caught her attention. It was almost like it beckoned her to pick it up.

The Bible she'd allowed to sit untouched for the past nine years. Why should she pick it up? At this point, God wouldn't want her to. Right?

A piercing agony crept into her bones, and she shivered. Her chin quivered as she tore her gaze away from the Bible. Instead of picking the Bible up, she grabbed the book about coaching employees and settled onto the sofa, determined to clear her mind of thoughts about anything but that big promotion.

Chapter 3

"What did you just say to me?" Keatyn took a hard gulp of her Mineral Water and stared across the table at Peter Brockton. Her eyebrows pinched so tight she could've been accused of having a unibrow.

The sunlight poured through the expansive window of Peter's modern dining room, casting a warm glow over everything it touched. The rich hue of his copper-red hair harmonized beautifully with his stylish Polo pullover and crisp khaki shorts.

He straightened his fork on the napkin. "I said that I think we should take a break."

She tilted her head and fixed Peter with a blank stare. "You can't be serious."

"You already know we aren't a good match, Keatyn." He gave a one-shoulder shrug. "You're just in denial."

"No. Peter, I don't." Her face hardened along with what had been left of her heart.

"Your friend Lucy shows more interest in me than you do." He shifted in his seat. "This is not what I signed up for."

Keatyn's eyes bulged, and her voice rose an octave. "So now we're getting somewhere. You want to date Lucy. I get it."

"That's not what I said." Peter hissed between clenched teeth. "I just said we should take a break."

Keatyn let out a bitter laugh. "You may as well have. Do you want her number, or do you already have it?"

"Stop it." He clenched his jaw tight as splotches of red trailed his neck and cheeks.

"All right. This is me. Stopping it." Keatyn jerked herself out of the chair before slapping her salad plate off the table. Lettuce and raspberry vinaigrette landed on the wall and slid to the hardwood floor.

"You're such a hateful person." Peter glanced at the salad on the floor and shook his head. "I hope someday you're able to find joy."

A heavy heat licked at Keatyn's skin, and she fought the urge to attack Peter physically. Instead, she grabbed her purse, slid on her oversized white sunglasses, and stomped out the front door. She pushed the gas pedal on her Infiniti and skidded out of the driveway, opening it up when she hit the highway.

She pulled over at a cliff a few miles down the road and slammed her fist into the steering wheel.

"I am not a hateful person." She massaged her temples. "I'm not hateful. I have joy."

Right?

Happy? She wracked her brain, trying to think about the last thing that truly made her happy. Well, there was the possible promotion. Yeah. There's that. Would a promotion be all it took to make Keatyn happy?

She punched the steering wheel again and immediately regretted it when a throbbing worked through her bones.

It's not like she went around lying or stealing. She didn't get involved in things other people do. She was a good person.

She had no doubt she would be going to Heaven. A sinking feeling hit her stomach, and it almost curdled. She *would* be going to Heaven.

Right?

An image of Peter and Lucy sharing a meal and laughing behind her back flashed through her mind. If she was going to Heaven when she died, then why did God leave her? Why did He allow Mama to die? And why would He allow the rest of her family to turn against her? They sided with the man who killed Mama. Why?

A tightening sensation hit Keatyn's chest, and she inhaled slow, steady breaths until it went away. If she refused God here and now, could she truly go to Heaven?

Maybe she needed to stop talking to herself about things she couldn't change. She must be losing it.

She needed to think about something else, like what kind of car she'd buy once she landed that promotion.

Keatyn took a few more deep breaths and slid her car into drive. She glanced down when her cell phone rang. Alvin. Probably to chew her out for hanging up on Myles. She declined the call. Right now, she needed no one but herself.

Chapter 4

All those late nights and hard work had finally paid off. Keatyn settled into her comfy office chair, admiring the items in her new workspace. The abstract paintings stood out beautifully against the dark mahogany furniture, creating an atmosphere of authority. A huge smile spread across her face as her chest filled with a sense of accomplishment and pride.

The crisp pinstriped black-and-white pantsuit screamed power. Everyone who walked by gave her a nod of respect. She couldn't help but laugh, filled with excitement about what was to come.

As the new Vice President of Westfield Financial, it was her time to show everyone what she was made of. They'd be following her rules. How could she not find happiness now?

Her desk phone beeped. She smiled and clicked the green button. "Yes, Amy?"

"Miss Griffin, your three o'clock appointment is here."

Keatyn glanced at her watch. Fifteen minutes early. That was a good sign. "Thank you, Amy. Give me ten minutes and send him in."

"Yes, ma'am."

An hour later, Keatyn's body hummed with excited energy. The first interview for Lucy's replacement had gone well. Now that she made the decisions, she needed loyal employees working directly under her. And that interview was a good start.

Keatyn's desk phone beeped again. "Yes, Amy?"

Amy's voice rang through the speaker with a nervous edge. "Miss Griffin, I'm sorry, but Lucy Parnell is here. I told her she couldn't see you without an appointment, but she insisted I ask."

"Send her in." A shrill of delight coursed through Keatyn. She was the boss, and it was time the team understood that. Especially Lucy.

Lucy burst through the double doors, red-faced and breathing hard. "Why are you transferring me to another office?" Black mascara smudged under Lucy's eyes and ran down her cheeks.

A sneer pulled at Keatyn's cheek. "I believe you can be useful at the Worthington branch."

Lucy's nostrils flared out to twice their size. "That branch is almost two hours from my house, Keatyn!"

"Please address me as Miss Griffin." Keatyn glanced down at her fingernails. "I can't have my employees accusing me of showing favoritism."

"You have got to be kidding me." A bitter laugh escaped Lucy's lips. "I thought we were friends."

Keatyn's lip twitched. "At least you have Peter."

"You didn't want him." Lucy's mouth hung slack briefly as if she needed a moment to gain her composure. "Don't you remember telling me to go for it when he asked me out almost six months after your breakup?"

"Of course I did. But you actually went out on a date with Peter. That's on you, Lucy. Not me." Keatyn snapped back.

"And I don't regret it! Peter is a wonderful man, Keatyn. Way too good for someone as cynical as you." Lucy's lips bunched together like she'd been sucking on a lemon.

Keatyn kept her expression neutral. "I told you–"

Lucy slammed her palm on Keatyn's desk. "My bad for thinking there was at least a little good left in you. Consider this my two-week notice, *Miss Griffin*."

Chapter 5

Keatyn glanced at her bowl of Frosted Flakes. She hated working from home but had to due to a headache that had worsened throughout the morning.

Ding. Ding. Her email goes off. Buzz. Buzz. Now her phone beeps. Message after message.

Was it possible for a phone to be a demon? Of course not.

She closed her laptop, her heart trembling as pins and needles traveled down her arms, landing at the top of her toes. She pulled her leg underneath her, thankful she'd not changed out of her comfy pajamas.

Pushing her head into the chair, she sighed. A piece of hair caught on the armrest, and she winced. It was past time for a good haircut. Her eyes drifted closed as she prayed for a moment's peace.

For the past ten years, she'd immersed herself in work. Her focus had always been getting as high up that corporate ladder as possible, and boy, she had succeeded. She still couldn't believe she'd been the Western Region Vice President at Westfield Financial for over a year now. She had the role of her dreams, yet nothing changed.

She'd been convinced that's what would make her happy. That's what would make her forget. It had worked for the first few months in the role.

She took a bite of her cereal. Her lips tugged downward as the bland flakes swished around in her mouth. What once was a treat now tasted like mushy cardboard. Thanks, stress.

She flipped her laptop open and stared at the computer screen. Buzz. Ding. Her heartbeat accelerated. Everything seemed so fake. Everything and everyone. Ever since Lucy left her life, she'd felt more alone than ever. Not that she could blame anyone but herself.

Why was she like this? What would it take for her to forget what happened to Mama? To her? What made Keatyn take her misery out on everyone else? Peter. Lucy. But especially God?

Misery had been her near-constant companion ever since that day. She longed to be happy but didn't quite know how. The pain behind her left shoulder blade intensified.

Why do the things that only a month before brought her pleasure now bring her sadness?

Why couldn't she forget?

Desperate to change her line of thinking, she scanned her phone for messages. Her heart dropped as Alvin's number jumped out at her.

She clicked on the message, and her throat knotted.

> *Hey, Sis. Dad's in the hospital. He's asked for you to come home. He wants to see you.*

> *Please.*

Keatyn's face heated. How dare he text her about that man. Her fingers lit up her iPhone keyboard.

> *No.*

> *Please. Dad may not make it much longer.*

> *No!*

> *He had a stroke. Your forgiveness is all he wants.*

> *I'll never forgive him.*

Keatyn pitched her phone inside her purse and snapped it shut. Her eyes rested on the bookcase on the other side of the room. Mama's Bible stared at her from the top shelf. Accusing her. Beckoning her. Could it be that she was strong enough to pick it up? Strong enough to see what Mama saw? To touch the pages she touched?

Keatyn drew in a deep breath and tiptoed over to the bookcase. She wrung her hands, and a hitch caught in her throat.

She grabbed the Bible, turned to a page Mama had marked, and closed it quickly. She placed it back on the top shelf and sank into her chair.

Pick it back up.

It's beyond time.

She darted her eyes back to the Bible.

Pick it up.

She moaned but gently picked the Bible up and flipped through the pages. It landed on a page in Ephesians. Mama had highlighted verses 31 and 32 of Chapter 4.

"Let all bitterness, wrath, anger, clamor, and evil speaking be put away from you, with all malice. And be kind to one another, tenderhearted, forgiving one another, just as God in Christ forgave you."

Right beside the verses, Mama had made a note that caused Keatyn's breath to hitch.

Put away wrath, or it will destroy you.

Why would Mama mark this page?

Could she have known that Keatyn would need to read these exact words.

Who was Keatyn to deny forgiveness to someone? No one, that's who. If Christ forgave, she could find the strength to forgive.

Couldn't she?

Guilt and shame surged through Keatyn's soul. She covered her face, standing on the brink of despair.

A spark of determination lit her features, igniting her resolve to change her way of thinking. Even if it meant transforming the person she had become.

Chapter 6

PENSACOLA, FLORIDA

Keatyn pulled into a spot at the Fort Hill church of Christ, the morning sun bouncing off her Toyota Camry.

Even though she had plenty of time after her flight from Seattle, sleep hadn't come. After tossing and turning for what felt like ages, she finally got up and made some coffee, enjoying a beautiful sunrise that barely softened the weight on her mind.

Now, as she prepared to walk inside, waves of anxiety and old memories hit her. Her hand shook on the steering wheel, bracing for what was about to unfold.

A woman in a blue Chevy Traverse waved at her as she walked into the church, making Keatyn's nerves kick up a notch. The woman's short blonde hair landed right above her shoulders, which suited her face. The purple and red floral maxi dress completely covered her full figure.

Keatyn gasped, the lump in her throat threatening to choke the breath out of her. Did she not recognize Keatyn? Not that Keatyn would expect her to. It had been ten years. She started the engine and shifted the gear into reverse.

Before she could back out, a familiar face appeared in the window. Alvin's short-sleeved blue and yellow button-up and light brown tweed pants pulled the blue out of his eyes and made them sparkle. "Keatyn? Is that really you? What are you doing? Are you leaving?" He didn't even attempt to hide his shock.

Keatyn rolled the window the rest of the way down, and the corner of her lip turned upward. "Hi, Alvin."

Alvin's lips tugged downward. "So, you were leaving? Church hasn't even started yet, Sis."

She shook her head but slipped the car back into park. "I can't do it, Alvin. I just can't."

Alvin opened the door and leaned around Keatyn, turning the car off and taking the keys. "You made it this far. Please come in."

Her brow furrowed as she held her hand out for the keys. "Is your father here?"

Alvin slapped her hand away. "*Our* father is still in the hospital. Sis, he's not doing well at all." His jaw ticked. "The stroke has impaired his speech and movement on one side of his body."

"Hmm." Keatyn aimed her eyes at the front entrance. It stared back at her, daring her to come in. "Listen, I'm going back to my condo in Navarre Beach. Can you stop by after service is over?"

"Nope." Alvin shook his head and stuck the keys to her rental in the pocket of his slacks. He backed out of Keatyn's reach and stuck his tongue out.

Keatyn leaned out the window and raised her voice. "Give me the keys. Right now."

Alvin smiled as he made his way to the front of the building. He turned around and waved at her as he walked backward through the double doors.

Keatyn silently screamed but got out of the car. She speed-walked as fast as her light blue pencil skirt and three-inch heels would allow to where Alvin stood. "Give me my keys, Alvin. This isn't funny. At all."

Tanya Willis handed Keatyn a bulletin, "Hello and welcome. Please take this bulletin and let us know if– " Her blue eyes grew wide, and her voice broke. "Keatyn?"

Keatyn grimaced. This was not how she wanted their reunion to work out. "Hello, Aunt Tanya."

"Oh, honey." Aunt Tanya's thick arms wrapped Keatyn in a suffocating hug. "I'm so happy to see you." Tanya handed Alvin the stack of bulletins, "Alvin, fill in for me as door greeter. Keatyn and I need to step into the ladies' room."

Tanya shut the door behind Keatyn and cupped her face. "It's been so long since I've seen this beautiful face of yours. Honey, why have you kept yourself from us so long?"

"I, um–" Keatyn swallowed.

"You know your dad is sick and near death. What will you do if that man dies before you make peace with him? Huh?" Tanya's mouth slid into a frown.

Keatyn decided to have a staring contest with the toilet. Anything to keep from meeting Tanya's gaze. "I hadn't planned on making peace with him if you want to know the truth."

Tanya's arm flew to her hip. "Well, I hope the fact that you're here means you've thought better of that decision."

"I'm not certain yet." Keatyn stiffened her gaze and met Tanya's eyes head-on. "And I don't need you coming at me about it, either."

"You need somebody to help knock some sense into that thick skull of yours. Why have you taken yourself away from me? Ten years have passed, and you barely even call to check on us."

"Alvin has kept me posted, Aunt Tanya. You know I've been busy." Keatyn sighed, "Can we talk about this later?"

Tanya's eyes lit up, "Of course, we can. If you promise not to leave town without us talking first."

"I promise." Keatyn squeezed Aunt Tanya's hand.

"Good. Now, let's get into the auditorium. Bible class has probably already started. Your Uncle Rodney teaches the class. Oh, he's going to be so happy to see you."

A few minutes later, Keatyn settled into the pew beside Aunt Tanya. She barely heard Uncle Rodney instruct the class to turn to the book of John before she locked eyes with her high school sweetheart.

Holding a baby.

Chapter 7

As soon as church was over, Keatyn flew out of the auditorium and straight out the front door. The determination she had to be a more forgiving person flew out right along with her.

She couldn't even remember the sermon. Or who preached it.

Her eyes had remained glued to her phone after seeing Kyle with a baby.

This had to be a sign. She was too weak to do this. After being alone these past ten years, maybe it would be better for her to continue to be alone.

No one cared about her.

No one.

The door latched shut, and Keatyn made a beeline to her rental. She stopped short of opening the door and growled before passing it by.

Alvin had the keys, so there would be no escaping in her car.

Walking, it is. She had to get as far away from that church building and everyone inside as quickly as possible. She'd crawl if she had to.

Her stomach rumbled. She dug around in her bag but came up empty-handed. Not even a cracker.

Within three blocks, both of her big toes throbbed like someone had smacked them with a hammer. She sank on the nearest bench and pulled her black heels off. She guessed today wasn't the best day to wear those suckers. She rubbed her toes and slapped the bottom of her feet before taking off down the sidewalk barefoot. It only took a few seconds for her to move over to the grass. What degree was it, anyway?

Sweat dripped off her nose as the sun peeked out from behind the lone cloud in the sky with a vengeance. Of course, she didn't have a hat. And her sunglasses were in the car.

The sweat kept coming no matter how many times she wiped it off. She'd give anything for a pool. Or a sprinkler. Or even a mud puddle.

Her lips quirked a tad as she finally took in the setting. She picked up the pace to get to the park where she played as a child. It was only a couple of blocks away. And there was a water fountain there.

Another block down the road, Alvin pulled over, holding a bottle of water out the window. "What's going on with you?"

Keatyn grabbed the water and took a long swig, nodding her thanks.

Alvin slid out of his pearl white Toyota Tacoma. "Why'd you leave?"

"This was a terrible mistake, Alvin." A pained look briefly crossed her face. "It's not just that man I don't want to see. I don't want to see anyone from my past."

A dog barked across the street, and its owner waved as he passed by. Alvin waved at the man and then turned back to Keatyn. "That sounds ridiculous. Why would you say that?"

"Because it's true. These people weren't here for me when Mama died, and I have no use for them." She shook her head, and her lips drew together. "None."

Alvin pinned Keatyn with a glower. "You have got to be the most selfish human I've ever met. You're my sister, and I love you, but man, you're something else."

Keatyn stared at Alvin slack-mouthed. "Me? Seriously? I'm selfish? That's the pot calling the kettle black."

"What do you mean, Keatyn?" Alvin tilted his head and tapped his chin. "Oh, you must be talking about how selfish I was when I left Dad alone after Mama died? Is that it?"

Keatyn glared at Alvin before reaching inside his truck for the napkin on his dashboard. She wiped her face, her mind working for a way to leave Pensacola like nothing ever happened.

Alvin continued, "Or do you mean when I left my sibling alone to help Dad deal with his grief? Not only his grief for losing Mama but over losing a child?"

"Stop it." Keatyn rubbed behind her ears. Her head may explode if it didn't stop pounding.

"What am I doing?" He threw his hands up. "Just trying to figure out what you mean when you say I'm selfish. Explain to me what you're referring to."

Keatyn stepped closer to Alvin with her fists clenched into tight balls. "I said stop talking."

Alvin rolled his eyes and pointed to the passenger seat. "Get in the truck, Keatyn. I'll give you a ride to the church building."

Keatyn opened the passenger door and leaned in. "You left me all alone after Mama died. You chose THAT MAN over me. That's how you're selfish." She jerked the door closed, instantly regretting it when her head throbbed with the sound.

"Stop acting like a child." He let out a deep breath. "Man, this blame game is getting old."

"Tell me about it." She turned to the window, refusing to look at Alvin. "Just take me to my car. I'm going home to Seattle."

"Fine. That's just fine. I have no idea how you made it all the way up to Vice President in your company. They must not know you act like a spoiled brat. If it ain't about you, you don't want nothing to do with it."

Fire shot from her eyes. "Stop talking and drive. I'm not kidding."

He shrugged and turned his attention to the road. After a few seconds, he turned to Keatyn. "How about we change the subject? Did you notice Kyle at church?"

Keatyn cut her eyes over at Alvin. "That's something else I'm not discussing."

"Oh. Right. Right." Alvin's jaw twitched. "Anything that makes Keatyn uncomfortable is off-limits. Would hate to make the center of the Universe feel any sort of way."

Sweat dripped down Keatyn's flushed face and neck, and she wiped the sweat onto her arm. "Do me a favor and keep your mouth shut."

Alvin drove in silence until he slid into the parking lot. He glanced over, and concern skirted across his face. He lowered his voice and put his hand out. "Hey, Keatyn. I'm sorry–"

"Just give me my keys and leave me alone." She said as she stepped out of the truck. She glanced down at the ground so intently you'd think she found a wad of money.

His face wore an expression of worry. "Sis–"

The world spun along with Keatyn's head. "I can't take this right now, Alvin. I feel like I'm about to have a heat stroke. Please. Give me my keys and let me go."

Alvin tossed Keatyn the keys, but they landed on the ground. She sighed and bent down to pick them up. Black stars clouded her vision, and she lost her balance. Looked like she'd be eating concrete for lunch.

Chapter 8

A cool sensation covered Keatyn's forehead like a soft ice pack. She lay there pretending to be out. Dreading another fight with Alvin.

Maybe she should get the inevitable over with.

Keatyn cracked open her eyes, and instead of meeting Alvin's blue eyes, she met a pair of eyes so brown they could almost be called black.

"How are you feeling?" Black eyes had a voice that caused a few tiny flutters to pass through her heart.

"What happened?" Keatyn blinked a few times as she looked at the surroundings. Wood blinds covered the windows, which flowed well with the stark white walls. They gave the place a masculine look that she appreciated.

Black eyes handed her a bottle of water. "Take a few sips of this. Don't gulp it down even though you may want to."

"Thank you." She took a sip of the water. She inwardly groaned as it coated her throat. She'd label it as the best water she'd ever had.

"You got too hot and fainted." Alvin touched her left shoulder. "I brought you here since it's right by the church."

Keatyn lost her breath when black eyes stood up. His short black hair and tan skin matched his eyes perfectly. Even though he wore a tan suit, white dress shirt, and baby blue tie, he looked like a marine who spent most of his time outdoors.

Three words came to Keatyn's mind. Masculine. Strong. Beautiful.

Don't go there. She was not looking for romance. Not after the fiasco with Peter.

Black eyes cleared his throat. "I'll give you two some privacy. Holler if you need anything."

Alvin stood and put his hand out. "Thank you, preacher man."

"Anytime, Alvin." He said as he grasped Alvin's hand.

"Wait." Keatyn shifted her weight on the leather sofa. "What's your name?"

He turned to Keatyn, his eyes bright yet kind as he spoke. "My name is Gareth Davenport."

Keatyn furrowed her brows as disappointment threatened to overtake her. "And you're the preacher?"

A grin appeared on his face. "Yes, ma'am."

Keatyn's stomach tightened. "All right. Thank you."

Since when do preachers look like that? Aren't they supposed to be older men with big noses?

No matter how attractive she found Gareth, Keatyn dismissed him as another fake—someone else to mislead and lie to and then claim to be a Christian.

In her mind, Alvin was the only Christian she'd ever been able to halfway count on.

"You're very welcome. I hope you feel up to joining us for evening service."

Keatyn's shoulders flinched. "Yeah, that's not likely," she muttered, inner turmoil evident in her voice.

Mama would be ashamed of Keatyn for talking to a preacher like that. Shouldn't she at least be nice? She forced a small smile. "But thank you for the offer. And for letting me rest here." Keatyn glanced around the room and threw her hand up. "Wherever here is."

"It's the parsonage. My home these past two years." Gareth paused in the doorway and met her wary gaze. "Keatyn, I hope you know how much the Lord loves you. How much He wants you to come home. Please let me know if I can help you. In any way."

"Doubt it." Keatyn mouthed under her breath.

Alvin took the seat Gareth vacated and handed her another water bottle. "Sis, I'm sorry for what I said earlier. The way I acted was not the way a Christian should ever act. Will you forgive me?"

Keatyn waved her hand dismissively. "Of course. I'm sorry, too. Coming here has my stomach in knots."

Alvin ate a handful of peanuts from the side table. "Don't you think it's time to face your fears? To tackle your past head-on?"

She sucked a breath in and held it for a second. Doubt and fear nearly overtook her senses. She exhaled and shook her head back and forth. "It's no good. I'm not ready."

"You'll never be ready at the rate you're going. But you're here. You've come this far, so why not see it through?" Alvin's determination shone through his hopeful eyes, the same eyes that had always been her undoing when they were younger. He knew how to get his way.

Her sight line drifted past Alvin and out the window, landing on a large palm tree in the yard. "I'm not strong enough, Alvin," she admitted, her vulnerability seeping through her words.

"Not alone, no, you're not." He turned her chin and met her eyes. "But you're not alone."

She met his gaze before focusing on the palm tree. "I know. I have you."

"Not me, Sis. Well, at least not me, primarily. You'll always have me, but most importantly, you have Christ."

The palm tree looked better and better. "You may have Christ, but Alvin, I don't. He left me ten years ago."

"Yes, you do. Christ never left you." Alvin leaned over, blocking the palm tree. "You're the one who left Him. He, on the other hand, will never forsake you."

Keatyn sipped her water. "I don't think–"

"You need faith."

Keatyn pulled the water bottle up to her mouth with trembling hands. "I don't know how Alvin. I don't."

Alvin stood up. "I'll be right back."

A few minutes later, he returned with Gareth trailing behind him.

A grin split Alvin's face wide. "Gareth has agreed to study with you."

Keatyn gave Alvin a death stare. "I didn't ask to study."

Gareth met Keatyn's smirk with a kind smile. "I'd be honored to study with you at any rate. Tell you what, we can talk first, then you can decide."

Alvin turned a pleading gaze on Keatyn. Again. "Come on, Sis."

She rolled her eyes. "Fine."

"You just made me so happy." Alvin pulled her into a hug. "Now, do you want to go see Dad?"

Keatyn turned a dark gaze on Alvin.

He raised his hands in surrender. "Okay. One step at a time, then."

Chapter 9

A few hours later, Keatyn rolled her window up as she turned left on Fort Picken's Road. Her heart rate increased when the pier came into sight. Her stomach twisted with mixed emotions. Why had she stayed away from this place so long?

A fragrant trail of suntan oil, warm and inviting, mingled with the intoxicating aroma of freshly fried fish and the tang of saltwater as she made her way toward the pier. With each step, her heart raced, thumping rhythmically in her chest, an eager drumroll building to a crescendo by the time she reached the end.

Lifting her face skyward, she inhaled deeply, allowing the familiar scents to envelop her like a comforting embrace, sun-kissed, and vibrant. No matter how far she traveled, nothing compared to this place. Memories of her past life seemed to be woven into every grain of sand and crashing wave.

As the waves broke against the sand, they carried her mind back to the carefree days of her youth. Back to sun-drenched afternoons filled with laughter and love. She could almost hear the echoes of joy from those times. She'd taken many romantic strolls with Kyle while Mama watched them, her feet splashing in the water, a book on her lap.

Though Mama's eyes were often glued to the pages, she always cast a watchful glance in their direction, keeping a protective eye on Keatyn and Kyle.

Double K, they liked to call themselves.

A brown pelican soared effortlessly by with its wings outstretched as it scanned the shimmering water below for its next meal. Keatyn raised her hand in a cheerful wave. Her heart raced as she quickly surveyed the bustling pier, wanting to ensure that no one had witnessed her moment of playful spontaneity. Across the dock, a little boy looked her way, his face lighting up with a bright, infectious smile. Captivated by his joy, she felt herself break into a genuine smile in return, her earlier embarrassment fading away.

After the disastrous moment she agreed to study with the preacher, she'd showered and changed into a flowing green sundress. Though there was a pier by her rental in Navarre, it held none of the cherished memories that this one did.

"Well, hello again, Miss Griffin." The preacher called out as he walked up the pier. He'd changed into khaki shorts that fell below his knees, a light green t-shirt, and brown Doc Martens sandals. No one would ever mistake Gareth for a tourist. That's for sure. He held a little girl's hand that could've been described as his mini-me based on her outfit.

Keatyn turned and put her hand up to her neck. "Oh, hello."

"I didn't expect to run into you here." Gareth cocked his head to the right. "We missed you at evening service."

"I could say the same thing." She forced a smile to her face. "Well, except for the missing you at the evening service part."

The little girl tugged on Gareth's shirt. Eyes the color of Gareth's blinked up at him. "Who's that, Daddy?"

He leaned down, and his lips spread wide, displaying deep dimples. "This is Mr. Alvin's sister."

The little girl's brow furrowed. "I didn't know Mr. Alvin had a sister."

Keatyn leaned down, and a genuine smile appeared on her face. "I'm Keatyn. What's your name?"

"My name is Wiiiweee." Another little girl waved, and Lily bounced on her toes. "Can I pwease go pway with my friend?"

"Yes, you may." He watched as she skipped up to her friend before turning back to Keatyn. "Her name is Lily, if you missed that. We've been working on our L sounds."

"I figured as much." Keatyn leaned against the pier.

"Lily was my brother's daughter."

"Oh, okay. It's nice that you get to spend time with her." Keatyn arched a questioning eyebrow. "I'm surprised she calls you Daddy then."

Gareth's gaze remained steady, his voice unwavering as he shared, "Lily and I are a team. I've raised her since she was a few months old."

Keatyn cocked her head as she took in that bit of information. "I don't mean to pry, but where's your brother?"

A dark cloud passed over Gareth's face. "He was killed on his first tour of duty with the Navy."

Keatyn blushed and bit her lip. "I'm sorry to hear that. I shouldn't have been so nosy."

"No, it's fine. And before you ask, her mother signed custody of Lily over to me and ran off after my brother died."

"Wow." Keatyn gazed at Lily as she and the other little girl played with dolls. "How do you stay so positive after all that? You seem to be happy."

Gareth's black eyes gazed deep into Keatyn's sea-green ones. "I *am* happy. There's a God in Heaven Who loves me. What right do I have to be anything but happy after all He's done for me?"

Keatyn squeezed her eyes shut and rubbed behind her ear. "Must be nice to feel loved."

Why made Keatyn say that out loud? One of these days, she'd learn to keep her thoughts to herself. "Listen, I shouldn't have said that. I think it's best if I get to my condo."

Gareth held up his hand, "I hope you aren't planning on backing out of our study."

Keatyn swallowed and ogled another bird as it flew by. "I'm not sure what to do. Part of me wants to go back home. A much smaller part thinks I should stay here. At least for my brother, if nothing else."

"Tell you what, I'll be in my office at eight in the morning. How about you meet me there between eight and nine? Study with me one time before you make up your mind. Okay? The church secretary comes in at seven, so we'll have someone there with us."

Keatyn hesitated, and the words Mama had written in her Bible echoed through her mind.

Put away wrath, or it will destroy you.

Her gaze locked into his. "Can you meet on Wednesday? If so, I'll be there. But I'll only commit to the one study."

A wide smile spread across Gareth's face, causing his dimples to be even more pronounced if that was possible. "I'm looking forward to our study on Wednesday morning, Miss Griffin." He held his hand out.

She grasped his hand in a firm shake, and her lips twitched to an almost smile. "Call me Keatyn."

"See you Wednesday morning, Keatyn."

"Please tell Lily I said it was nice meeting her."

"Will do. Have a good night."

Keatyn made her way down the pier, her mind in turmoil. What just happened? Why did she agree to meet him for a Bible study?

Because he'd suffered loss just like her.

He seemed content. Could he, in turn, help her find a semblance of happiness? As Keatyn drove onto Gulf Boulevard, a weight lifted from her heart.

Chapter 10

Keatyn took one last look at her sporty trousers and thin sweater vest before pulling on the double doors to the church building at eight on the dot. Maybe she should've worn a dress or slacks. Not that it mattered – it was too late to stress over clothes. What she had on would have to do.

After walking through the foyer, she glanced inside the office she played in as a child. Thoughts of playing hide-and-seek with her old friend Rebecca caused a smile to sneak across her face.

An older woman with grayish-blue hair sat behind the desk. "Good morning, my dear. You must be Keatyn Griffin." She beamed a smile before raising her voice a few octaves. "I'm Cordelia Inman, the church secretary. Come right in. Gareth's expecting you."

The woman's smile turned out to be contagious. "Good morning, Miss Inman."

Gareth emerged from the office directly across the hall, exuding an almost otherworldly charm that reminded Keatyn of a merman. Clad in a loose teal button-up shirt that fluttered slightly with his movements and black slacks, he could have easily been a model for any high-end brand. "Good morning," he greeted Keatyn with a friendly smile. "Please, come on in. I trust you had a restful night?"

"Yes, good morning." Keatyn stepped into the office and pulled the door closed behind her.

Gareth cleared his throat as he propped the door back open. "Let's leave the door open, please. Miss Cordelia won't be able to hear anything we say. Believe me."

Keatyn shrugged as her eyes went straight to the wall of bookcases to the right of the massive oak desk. The only wall without bookcases held a large map of the world. She thought the office fit the style Gareth portrayed.

Across the hall, Cordelia mumbled something about not being able to believe she had forgotten her hearing aids. Keatyn pressed her hand across her mouth to keep from bursting out laughing.

"See?" Gareth's laughter came out deep and somehow light at the same time. Despite his profession, a slight stir settled in Keatyn's stomach.

What in the world was that?

A glint remained in his eyes. "Now that the ice is broken, how about we get coffee and start our study?" His inviting tone caused Keatyn's stiff spine to relax.

He poured them both a cup before settling into the chair behind the desk. "Do you have any questions before we start?"

Keatyn nodded and scrunched her lips, her gaze landing on the ceiling. "I would like to know for real if you're truly as happy as you portray, or is it just for show? You know, since you're the preacher?"

He answered her question with another question. "Keatyn, do you believe in God?"

"Yes. Of course, I believe in God." Keatyn answered the question slowly, almost like speaking to a three-year-old.

"All right." Gareth propped his elbows on his desk and entwined his hands. "But do you believe God?"

Keatyn cocked her head to the left, her mind racing for the answer. "What's the difference?"

"Many people believe in God, but few believe what God says." He paused before emphasizing the following two words. "Do you?"

She crossed her long legs, stiffened her back, and met Gareth's gaze. "He's not a liar if that's what you're asking."

His head bobbed up and down as he twiddled with an invisible hair on his chin. "Why do you think Christ died?"

A spasm ticked in her throat. This was not the conversation she wanted to have. Wasn't he supposed to show her how to be happy? His eyes never left hers as he seemed to await her answer patiently. It wasn't a hard question to answer. Everyone knew why Christ died. "For our sins."

His tan fingers flipped through the Bible on his desk. "But why would He do that? Turn to Romans 5:8, and read with me."

"But God demonstrates His own love toward us, in that while we were still sinners, Christ died for us."

He rested his elbows on the desk and shifted his body closer to the desk. "What does this verse say to you?"

Keatyn glanced at the Bible app on her phone screen. "It's pretty simple. Right? It means God loves us so much that Christ died for our sins."

He relaxed into the chair and gave her a look that almost made her feel guilty for thinking about her own happiness. "Let's make it personal. God loves **me** so much that Christ died for **my** sins."

Keatyn stared at Gareth with a guarded expression, the tension in the conversation palpable. "Just because He died for my sins doesn't mean He hasn't left me alone to deal with everything."

"Why do you think God has left you alone?" His voice carried a warmth and concern that wrapped around her like a comforting blanket.

Keatyn sighed softly, picking a stray piece of fuzz off her pants. "He just has," she replied quietly, avoiding his gaze. "I don't want to talk about it right now."

"Do you think the Bible suggests that we'll never face suffering?" he continued gently, encouraging her to open up.

Keatyn furrowed her brows as she considered his question. "I don't think it says that at all," she finally admitted, a hint of uncertainty in her voice.

"John 16:33 tells us that we will. Let's read it together."

"These things I have spoken to you, that in Me you may have peace. In the world you will have tribulation; but be of good cheer, I have overcome the world."

Gareth locked eyes with Keatyn. "In this world, what can we expect?" he asked, his voice steady.

"Tribulation," she replied, her gaze momentarily drifting to the steam rising from her coffee cup.

He leaned forward slightly, a furrow of concern forming on his brow. "Do you think that means God doesn't love us? That He turns His back on us during our times of suffering?"

She paused, carefully sipping her coffee, weighing her thoughts. "I'm not sure," she murmured.

With a deep breath, Gareth continued, "When we began this conversation, you asked me if I was truly happy. Again, I feel I have no right to dwell in unhappiness. God loves me deeply. He sacrificed His only begotten Son for my sins. Who am I to challenge His plan?" His words hung between them.

"You're stronger than I am. That's something I can't deny," Keatyn said, a hint of sadness in her voice. She briefly looked at her phone, its screen lighting up with an incoming email notification. "Oh no, I have a call in fifteen minutes. Can we continue this discussion later?"

Gareth leaned against the desk, his brow slightly furrowed. "Are you free this afternoon, or would you prefer tomorrow morning?"

"I think this afternoon will work best," she replied, scrolling through her calendar, her fingers pausing momentarily. "How about three o'clock? Does that work for you?"

"Absolutely. I'll see you back here at three," Gareth said with a nod, a reassuring smile spreading across his face.

Chapter 11

A gentle but warm breeze rustled the leaves above as Keatyn settled onto a sun-drenched bench at the park, just a few blocks from the church building. Luckily, she could work remotely and had an excellent Assistant Vice President who could handle most things without her.

As she prepared for the call, memories of her carefree childhood rushed back, vivid as ever. She could almost hear her mother's laughter as she pushed Keatyn on the colorful merry-go-round, the rhythmic squeak of the metal bringing joy to Keatyn's heart.

She recalled her father's encouraging words, urging her to conquer the big kid's slide and how she had finally scrambled to the top. Years later, she had done the same for her little brother, Alvin, the pride swelling in her chest as he slid down for the first time.

She'd just ended the conference call when her phone vibrated. She hit the answer button. "Hey, Alvin."

"Hey there, Sis." He let out a sigh. "I need to talk to you in person."

Uh oh.

"I'm at our favorite childhood park. Do you want to come here? Or meet somewhere else?"

"I can be there in less than ten minutes."

"I'll be here." Keatyn laid her phone on the picnic table and sat on a swing.

A squirrel scurried down the side of a tree before hopping onto the ground. It glanced at Keatyn before tearing off in the opposite direction. Her eyes crinkled with a smile as the squirrel disappeared behind another tree. If only she could be so carefree, even for a while.

Alvin hopped out of his Tundra a few minutes later and motioned for Keatyn to join him on the bench.

Her feet dangled as the swing moved back and forth. "What's up?"

The look on his face made Keatyn want to turn around and run in the other direction. Instead, she hopped out of the swing and plopped down beside him. "What's wrong?" A frog hitched in her throat. "Is it Dad? Did he die?"

"No, it's not that." Alvin rubbed the back of his neck and glanced at Keatyn. "Dad's all set up to come home in a few days. He has a bed, and a home health nurse will come for several hours a day."

"And why does that not make you happier?" Keatyn screwed her face up. "Last I heard, you thought he was on the verge of death."

Alvin tugged at his shirt collar. "That's not the part I'm worried about."

Keatyn's skin turned clammy. "Oh? What is it then?"

Seconds ticked by before Alvin spoke. "Guess there's no point in putting it off."

"Okay, now you're scaring me." Keatyn pecked her thumb on her leg. "What's going on? Just tell me."

"I just got off the call with my Commander. I'm being deployed."

Her heart missed a beat as Alvin's words sunk in. "Please tell me you're kidding."

He shrugged. "I can't. You know what that means, right?"

"That I came here and won't even get to see you for how long? Three months?" Keatyn gulped down the last of her water.

"Yep, I leave in seven days." He rested his hand on Keatyn's shoulder.

Keatyn stiffened and shrugged his hand off her shoulder. "Well, at least we get to spend a few days together before you go."

He squared his shoulders before hopping off the table. "Dad's gonna need you to stay with him while I'm away."

"No."

"He's coming home in a couple of days. I'll get him settled and taken care of the first few days, but that's all I can do before I leave."

A Lexus SUV pulling into the parking lot completely caught Alvin's attention. Keatyn followed his gaze, and when a woman who could play the lead in a Pocahontas film stepped out of the vehicle, Keatyn understood. She opened the back door, and two kids bounced out of the car.

She stopped at the picnic table and smiled. "Hi, Alvin."

"Hello, Sylvia and kiddos." Alvin's face heated up. "This is my sister, Keatyn."

Sylvia's smile broadened as she pulled her chocolate hair into a bun. "Oh. Hi Keatyn, I'm Sylvia, and those two hoodlums running toward the swings are my four-year-old twin boys, Oakland and Rhyland."

Alvin drummed his fingers on the picnic table. "Sylvia, I was planning to call you later. Can you meet me at the Red Snapper restaurant for a quick dinner one night this week?"

"Sure, I'll see what night mom can watch the kids and let you know." Sylvia pinned Keatyn with her gaze. "Nice to meet you, Keatyn."

Keatyn glanced back and forth between Sylvia and Alvin. Could it be baby brother has a girlfriend?

"You, too." Keatyn waited for Sylvia to get to the swing set before turning to Alvin. "Call your commander and tell him you have a family emergency."

"That's not how things work." He spoke to Keatyn, but his eyes remained on Sylvia as she pushed the boys on the swing set.

"Why not? You do have an emergency." Keatyn snapped her fingers. "I'm talking to you."

"But I also have a sister who can fill in. I won't do that to my team. I'm deploying. So, you need to step up."

Keatyn inspected her fingernails. "Dad probably won't even want me to."

"That's where you're wrong. He does."

"No." Keatyn shuddered. This is not what she signed up for.

"Keatyn. I'm going to need you to snap out of it." Alvin glanced at Sylvia again.

"I shouldn't have come back to this place," Keatyn said, her insides quaking like she'd been on an amusement park ride.

"Yes, you should have." He lowered his voice. "I don't know what I'd do if you weren't here. Please help with Dad."

"Alvin–"

"Please. I've not once asked you for anything these past ten years. Do I have to beg?"

Keatyn gasped. That's the nicest way she'd ever been called selfish. "I'll do it. For you."

A wide grin spread across his face, and he jerked Keatyn into a bear hug. "Thank you. This means so much, and I can't wait to tell Dad."

Keatyn returned Alvin's smile, but deep inside, her only thought was, what had she done?

Chapter 12

Cordelia Inman cracked a grin at Keatyn. "I had to go home on lunch and get my hearing aids. I can't believe I forgot them this morning. I'm only sixty-five. Way too young to be so forgetful."

"I can relate to being forgetful." Keatyn pointed at the closed door. "Is Mr. Davenport in? I was supposed to be back at three today."

"Mr. Davenport? That's what they called my dad. Please call me Gareth." Gareth's deep voice echoed down the hallway as the front door snapped shut behind him.

Keatyn raised an eyebrow. "Only if you call me Keatyn. No more Miss Griffin."

"It's a deal. Sorry if I'm late. I just dropped Lily off at her grandma's from preschool." Gareth held Keatyn's gaze.

"No need to apologize." Keatyn broke eye contact and swallowed the lump in her throat. "You're not late. I'm a bit early."

Cordelia's gaze went from Gareth to Keatyn, and she puckered her lips. "You two better get to it. I'll be right in here if you need anything."

"Yes, ma'am." Gareth's eyes slid to Keatyn. "You ready to begin?"

Even though her heart kicked up a notch, Keatyn managed to nod.

They settled into their seats before Gareth spoke. "I trust your call went well."

Keatyn crossed her legs. "Yes, it did."

Cordelia strolled into the office with two bottles of water. "In case you get thirsty."

Gareth took the water and turned thankful eyes on Cordelia. "Thank you."

Keatyn smiled at Cordelia. "Yes, thank you. That was so thoughtful."

Gareth set the water down on the desk. "Do you have any questions before we begin?"

Keatyn shook her head. "Not that I can think of."

Gareth took a swig of water and rubbed his chin. That must be his go-to when he's studying. "When Adam and Eve sinned in the garden, God felt such a great loss. He desired we return to Him, but He would have to suffer another loss. His only begotten Son." He flipped through his Bible. "Let's turn over to First John chapter 4, verse 9."

"In this the love of God was manifested toward us, that God has sent His only begotten Son into the world, that we might live through Him."

Gareth's eyes locked onto Keatyn's, a mix of intensity and care in his gaze. "What happened to Jesus when He was on the earth? At the end?"

Rubbing her arms, her mouth turned slightly downwards into a frown. "A lot happened to Jesus while He was here. But at the end, He was hung on the cross."

"Why?" he pressed, seeming eager for her to delve deeper.

"Because of sin." She replied, her voice tinged with sadness.

"What would cause Jesus to do that, though? Let's go over the verse again."

After reading the verse over, Keatyn bit her bottom lip. "Love for us."

Gareth leaned across the desk, making the moment seem more personal. "With that being said, how much does God love us? Ask yourself this, Keatyn. How much does God love you?"

Keatyn shifted uncomfortably in her chair, a warm flush creeping up her neck as she controlled her emotions. "He loves me more than I can comprehend," she said, her voice barely above a whisper.

"That's one way to look at it. He loves us more than words can say. So much that He suffered the loss of His Son for us. This, in turn, teaches us about forgiveness."

Keatyn knitted her eyebrows together. "Why do you say that?"

"Because forgiveness is a sort of loss. You must lose your feelings against those you think wronged you to have them back in your life," Gareth explained, his tone gentle yet firm.

"Do you even know what happened to my mama?" Keatyn shot back, her words laced with a sharp edge.

"I know your entire family suffered from the tragic fire that took your mama." His shoulders sagged. "I'm more sorry than I can express."

"Did you know that Myles left Mama in the house so he could get Alvin and me out?" Her voice quivered as she glared at Gareth.

"I know Myles made a choice that he's had to live with these past ten years."

"He didn't even try to go back in there." Keatyn rubbed her temples and took a deep breath. The tension in her chest threatened to shatter her composure.

"Don't you think he's had to live with that just like you? That he has suffered just like you?" His facial expression slid into a slight frown.

"I have no idea." Keatyn rose abruptly, a storm of feelings swirling inside her. "I don't think a study is what I need right now. Thank you for your time."

Gareth sprung to his feet. "Keatyn, wait a minute."

She paused, her hand resting on the door handle. "My emotions are all over the place. Maybe now isn't the best time. I'm sorry if I caused your schedule to be off."

Gareth stepped closer. "This has nothing to do with my schedule. It has everything to do with your relationship with your Heavenly Father. I'll be right here when you're ready."

"You promise?" she asked as hope flickered within her.

"I promise," he replied, his sincerity grounding her spiraling thoughts.

Chapter 13

The following day, Keatyn shuffled down the long, sterile corridor of Pensacola General Hospital, each step heavy with reluctance. The sharp, clinical scent of ammonia mixed with bleach filled the air, clawing at the back of her throat and making her stomach churn. Instinctively, she tugged the neck of her sleeveless turtleneck up over her nose, desperate to shield herself from the biting odor lingering in the hallway.

Out of nowhere, a flaxen-haired nurse, her face partially concealed by a mask, stepped into Keatyn's path, halting her progress. "Keatyn? Keatyn Griffin? Is that really you?" the nurse called out, her voice ringing with a mix of surprise and nostalgia.

Keatyn froze, her heart racing. That familiar voice transported her back to a different time. As the nurse pulled her mask down, Keatyn was struck by the brilliance of her smile. Straight, white teeth framed a cheerful grin, punctuated by a single tooth that jutted out to the left, giving her an endearing charm that was hard to ignore.

"Rebecca McDonald. Wow."

Rebecca extended her arms, and Keatyn hesitated before stepping in for a hug. "I haven't seen you in forever."

"It's definitely been a while." A smile broke through Keatyn's tough exterior. "How have you been?"

Rebecca glanced towards the wall and said, "The Lord has truly blessed me. How about you? How you holding up?"

"Doing fine," Keatyn replied, looking around to see if anyone else was nearby.

Lowering her voice as if they were sharing a secret, Rebecca continued, "I heard you ended up staying in Washington."

As Keatyn listened to Rebecca, a wave of anxiety washer over her, sending tingles of nerves through her body. The thought of facing Myles felt daunting, leaving her heart racing. She wasn't ready for that moment. As she pondered the future, she couldn't help but wonder if she'd ever find the courage to confront him.

Rebecca cleared her throat, and Keatyn snapped back to attention. "Sorry. Yes, I settled down in Seattle after graduating from college. Got a job and been busy with work ever since."

"That's okay. I know you have a lot on your mind, especially worrying about your dad." Rebecca poked

Keatyn playfully with her elbow. "Alvin told Kyle that you're a big-time Vice President now."

"Living the dream." Keatyn half laughed. "And you always wanted to be a nurse."

"Yep. All I ever wanted was to take care of people." Rebecca gently touched Keatyn's wrist. "I was sorry to hear about your dad's stroke."

"Thanks," Keatyn said, scratching her foot through her sandal.

Rebecca's light touch shifted to a firm squeeze. "I hear he's going home soon, so that's good news."

"Well, it was good to see you. I'm going to go ahead and check on Myles."

Rebecca's eyes widened. "It was good to see you too. Don't be such a stranger."

"I won't," Keatyn said, waving as she walked away.

Why would Alvin tell Kyle about Keatyn's life? And why would Kyle tell Rebecca?

Continuing down the hall, she tiptoed to room 201, pausing outside the door. She inhaled a few breaths and put her hand on the door when voices echoed in the hall.

"I wish I could stay with you, Dad. But Keatyn will take good care of you while I'm away."

A barely legible sound came out a few times before Keatyn could make out the words. "No. She hates me."

"She doesn't hate you, Dad. And don't worry, even if Keatyn did hate you, she would never hurt you."

"Not that. Want her happy." Myles grunted like he was thinking hard about what words to use. "Not take care of me. She needs happiness. Love."

"Oh, Dad. If only Keatyn knew how much you love her."

"Love baby girl."

"I know she's your baby girl." Alvin sighed. "I think we should tell her–"

"No." Sobbing came from the room.

The air left Keatyn's lungs, and she jerked her hand away from the door.

How often had he tried to tell Keatyn that he loved her over the past ten years? More times than she could count. Yet, she never wanted to listen.

A heaviness filled her heart as Mama's face flashed in her mind. She leaned against the wall, staring at the ceiling. After a few moments, she glanced at the door before returning the way she came.

Only to slam into a hard chest.

Chapter 14

Keatyn lifted her gaze and locked eyes with Gareth. "Where's the fire?" Gareth's hands gently wrapped around Keatyn's arms, steadying her as he moved her away from the warmth of his chest.

"I'm sorry. I was... um..." Keatyn swallowed hard, the lump in her throat making it difficult to form a coherent thought. She averted her gaze, focusing intently on the floor. "I needed to go that way." With a hesitant gesture, she pointed down the dimly lit hallway, her cheeks burning with embarrassment.

Gareth glanced in the direction she pointed before pinning her with his gaze. "Is everything okay?"

"Of course." Keatyn put on her best VP face.

"Have you already seen your dad?" Gareth peeked around her. "How's he doing today?"

Her throat bulged with a hard swallow. "No, I mean yes. I just realized I needed to be somewhere else."

Don't you dare lie to a preacher. She quickly chastised herself. However, it wasn't a lie. She did need to be somewhere else. Anywhere else but here.

Gareth stepped aside. "Well, if you're sure nothing's wrong. Try to have a good day, Miss Griffin."

Miss Griffin? What happened to Keatyn? Maybe he didn't call crazy people by their first names.

Uncle Rodney, Daniel Bradford, and Randall Patterson padded down the hall as Keatyn tried to maneuver around Gareth.

Great, now the elders would ask her a million questions. Who would show up next? Aunt Tanya?

"Hi there, Gareth. Keatyn." Randall smiled and tugged on his army green suspenders.

"Hello, I'm just on my way out." Keatyn croaked out as she walked away, rubbing the spots on her arms Gareth had touched.

Gareth paused at the entrance of the hospital room, glancing thoughtfully at Keatyn as she hurried down the hallway.

What's your story, Keatyn Griffin?

From the sound of things, Keatyn had stayed away ever since the death of her mother.

Gareth had always assumed she avoided Pensacola because she hadn't come to terms with her mother's death. Now, however, he realized there was more to it—she blamed her father. Reflecting on their past conversations, he concluded that had to be the reason.

Alvin had mentioned that she was a Christian but had left the church years ago. Had her heart grown too hard to return? No, anyone can turn back to God if they have the desire and the love. But did she? From her behavior, he believed she had the love, though she might not even realize it herself. Perhaps she needed a gentle nudge to discover it, someone to show genuine interest in her soul.

Gareth pecked on the door as he opened it. "Knock, knock." He smiled at Alvin. "Is Myles up to some company?"

Alvin lifted himself out of the chair beside the bed. "Hey, preacher man. It's good to see you."

The elders walked in behind Gareth, and after exchanging greetings, Myles lifted one side of his mouth to a lopsided grin. "Sit."

The elders declined to sit, but Gareth lowered himself into the recliner on the other side of the bed. He grasped Myles's hand. "It's good to see you doing better, Myles."

Myles's head bobbed up and down. "Yeah."

Gareth turned to Alvin. "What can we help with?"

"Well. I'm not sure." Alvin crossed his arms. "You know I got orders to deploy in a few days?"

"I hadn't heard." Gareth shot a glance at Myles from the corner of his eye. "What's that mean for Myles?"

Randall spoke up. "Do we need to arrange for the church members to take turns staying with him?"

Alvin's eyes glinted with a light that wasn't there before. "I don't know what to say. It would be amazing to get some help for Keatyn. Maybe give her breaks so she can work."

"Did your sister agree to stay?" Gareth asked, his brow arching in surprise. Rodney turned toward the door, a motion that couldn't quite mask the flicker of astonishment that had flashed across his face. Gareth briefly glimpsed his reaction, a knowing smile creeping onto his lips.

"She did."

"That's fantastic news," Gareth said, his voice warm with enthusiasm.

Alvin let out a half-grunt, half-laugh. "The jury's still out on that one."

Chapter 15

The door swung shut behind Keatyn with a definitive bang as she stormed into the condo, her energy reminiscent of a tornado tearing through a quiet neighborhood. Her cell phone buzzed from within her purse. She rummaged through makeup, receipts, and an assortment of odds and ends and came up empty-handed.

Growing increasingly frustrated, she flipped her purse upside down, scattering its contents across the sleek glass dining room table. A hairbrush rolled to the edge, and a stray lipstick tube clattered to the floor, but still, her phone was nowhere to be found.

Finally, her fingers brushed against the familiar shape of the device. She seized the phone, bringing it swiftly to her ear, her heart racing. It was no surprise to hear Alvin's calm voice on the other end, cutting through her whirlwind of thoughts.

"Hey, Alvin." She glided gracefully across the sunlit room, the floorboards creaking softly beneath her feet as she approached the sliding glass doors.

With a gentle push, the doors opened, and a warm breeze rushed in, carrying the unmistakable scent of salty sea air. She closed her eyes, letting the wind envelop her. The rhythmic sound of waves crashing against the shore filled her ears, a soothing symphony that contrasted with the chaos in her mind. Hearing Myles's voice had stirred emotions she had long buried, leaving her in a whirlwind of confusion and longing.

"Hey, Sis. Are you listening?"

"Sorry, yes. What did you say?"

"I said I thought you were coming by the hospital today."

"Change of plans."

Alvin let out a hmph. "Dad was looking forward to seeing you."

"Well, I'll see him when he gets home." Keatyn squinted to read an advertisement on an airplane as it cruised by. Something about fish tacos. "That'll probably be easier anyway."

"Easier on who? You?"

"Come on, Alvin. Please don't start. This is difficult enough."

"All right. All right. Listen, can you meet me at Dad's in an hour? I need to give you a key and the alarm code."

"I suppose. What's the address?"

"1119 Calle Bonita Way on Pensacola Beach."

"Wow. Right on the beach?"

"Yeah. Dad bought a fixer-upper when the market was slow. Got a great deal."

"Well, good for him." She fixed her gaze on a woman on a paddleboard.

"Sis –"

She stepped inside, pulling the door closed behind her. "I'm sorry. Still working on my attitude."

"That's a start. I'll see you in an hour."

"See you then." Her mouth watered with the thought of a juicy piece of fish." I'll bring fish tacos."

"Sounds good. And Sis?"

"Yeah?"

"Thank you for this. I love you."

"Love you, too, Bubba."

An hour later, Keatyn parked her rental car in front of a two-story house directly on the beach. The outside sported a color between teal and turquoise with white trim, a melon-orange door, and white shutters. The white stilts and decking flowed perfectly with the shutters.

Alvin leaned against his truck, talking on the phone. He hung up when Keatyn stepped out of her car. The corners of his mouth quirked into a smile. "Hi-ya!"

"Hey there." She nodded at the house. "This is actually adorable."

"Wait until you see the inside." He headed up the steps, looking back at Keatyn when he spoke. "It's a lot bigger than it looks."

She ran her hand down the railing and paused to take in the rolling waves. This had to be the best feeling ever. "I don't see how that's possible. It looks huge."

He unlocked the door and gestured for Keatyn to follow him inside. The interior surprised her with its uniqueness. Polished concrete floors gleamed in the sunlight, and an exposed brick wall added character to the space. However, the view was the highlight. Glass windows lined the entire back wall, with a sliding glass door in the center.

As waves crashed onto the shore, Keatyn let out a low whistle in admiration. She looked at the open ceiling, where dark beams spanned the living area and extended into the open kitchen. "Did Myles come into some money or something?" she asked.

Alvin scrunched his face up. "Dad's always made good money, Keatyn. But most of this stuff was bought at flea markets and antique stores. He bought two houses at auction, and we renovated them ourselves."

Her eyes turned round as saucers. "Two?"

Alvin headed past Keatyn and stopped at a window. "See the little cottage up there?" He pointed at a smaller house closer to the road.

Keatyn followed his gaze. "I do."

"That one's mine."

"I'm impressed." Keatyn crossed her arms. Not looking impressed.

A big, goofy grin split his face. "Dad'll be so happy that you like it."

Keatyn rolled her eyes. "Don't know why that would matter. It's his home, not mine."

He muttered something under his breath as he grabbed a couple of plates out of the cabinet. "Hand me a taco. My mouth's been watering ever since you brought them up."

Mesmerized by the waves, Keatyn didn't bother to move.

Alvin tapped his foot. "Come on, Sis. I have plans this evening and still have to get ready."

"Oooh. With Sylvia, maybe?" Keatyn jutted her eyebrows up and down. "Does baby bro have a sweetheart?"

"Hush up." He picked up a pillow off the sofa and threw it at Keatyn.

A laugh bubbled out of her chest. "Oh, you want some of this?" She picked up a pillow and plopped him upside his head. "Bring it on, baby brother."

Alvin grinned at Keatyn after taking a pillow beatdown. "All right. You're still the official champion of pillow fights."

She blew on her fingers. "Now, tell me about Sylvia."

"Can I have a taco first?"

"Absolutely." She handed a container to Alvin. "All that whooping on you caused me to be famished."

After the last fish taco was eaten, Alvin sighed. "She's not my sweetheart. Sylvia and her kids have been through a lot, and I'm just trying to be there for them."

Keatyn cocked her head to the right. "Spill."

"She lost her husband a little over a year ago." A dark sadness appeared on his face. "Do you remember my high school mentor, Lee Mason?"

"The football player you looked up to? Yes, of course, I remember him. He was a couple of years behind me. Where is he now?" She clamped a hand over her mouth as understanding dawned on her. "Wait, did he pass away?"

Alvin stared out the window, seemingly lost in thought. "He was shot, and his body went missing after he and his partner were investigating a string of kidnappings."

Keatyn's eyes bugged out, and her voice raised an octave. "Kidnappings? Here?"

Alvin raised his eyebrows. "The women were from another country, and Lee thought they were being forced to work. It looks like it was part of a bigger operation. I don't know all the details, though."

"If they didn't find Lee's body, what makes them think he's dead?" Keatyn glimpsed the tears in Alvin's eyes as he turned back to stare outside.

"The investigator determined the blood loss was too significant for him to have lived through it.

Keatyn leaned her head on Alvin's shoulder. "That's sad."

"Yes. So now you know why I want to be there for Lee's family. I think he would want me to. I honestly didn't realize I'd develop feelings for Sylvia."

Keatyn moved to pick up the pillows and straightened them on the sofa. "Are you in love with her?"

"I care about her. Not sure if it's love." Alvin licked his lips. "I've never felt that before. So, maybe?"

"I think you'd know if it were love." She met his gaze, doing her best to look confident. She wouldn't know love if it knocked her in the head.

"How do you know that? Are you in love with someone?" It was Alvin's turn to jiggle his eyebrows.

"Not at all." Keatyn raised a pillow above her head. "Now get out of here before I have to give you another beat down."

Chapter 16

Keatyn sat down on the cream sectional in Dad's living room. Then she stood up and rubbed her neck, feeling an all too familiar tension.

She took a sip of water, walked over to the sliding glass door, and quickly stepped onto the patio. The gloomy sky ranged from dark blue to light gray. A single white cloud drifted across the sky and reminded Keatyn of herself. Alone.

The waves crashing into the shore helped slow her excited breathing. A dark shadow crossed the sky, and within seconds, rain drenched her.

Usually, she'd escape to the dry house. But not today. Today, she needed this. This feeling of being alive as the rain pelted her face and stung her cheeks.

She thought about Alvin picking Myles up at the hospital and groaned. Nervous energy skidded through her stomach. She glanced at the beach, and an idea formed.

Should she? No way. She puckered her lips out and cocked her head. Why not? The rain had stopped, so what could it hurt?

She slipped out of her flip-flops and pranced to the shore, wading in until water reached her knees. She threw her hands in the air and let out a burst of giggles.

The clear water swirled around her, revealing a variety of shells. As she reached for an orange one, she slipped and fell. Spitting out seawater, she embraced her laughter.

As she stood, she scooped up a handful of sand, letting it trickle down her arm. Another wave crashed into her, knocking her down again. She crawled closer to the shore and sucked in a few breaths of air mingled with salt and rain.

Now, this is living. This right here. Why did she stay away so long?

She flipped onto her back and closed her eyes as another cloud passed, pelting her face with rain. Shivers tripped up her spine, and she embraced a burst of childlike laughter that had been missing from her life for far too long.

After what seemed like forever, she dragged herself to her feet and skipped back toward the house, spinning in a few circles. As the rain dwindled to a drizzle, she spun around once more and allowed a laugh to come full and free.

The shivers she experienced earlier turned into a patch of fire traveling up her neck as she met a pair of black eyes staring at her from the patio.

"I thought that was you out there, but Alvin said it couldn't be." Amusement bounced from his eyes.

Keatyn stepped onto the patio and wrung her hair out. "Yep."

Alvin leaned against the wall, holding his side with laughter when they walked into the room. He shot over to her and punched her shoulder. "I was NOT expecting to come home to that."

Keatyn shook her head and sprayed him with water. "I guess not." She gave him a sheepish smile.

Myles sat in his chair with tears in his eyes. He opened his mouth, and a slight sound came out. He shook his head and tried again. "Keeeattt." He raised his hand on his right arm and motioned for Keatyn to come close.

Shame spread throughout Keatyn as she inched toward Myles. "Hello."

A crooked smile seemed to be plastered on Myles's face. He held his hand out again, and this time, Keatyn took it. The words Mama had written in her Bible echoed throughout her mind for the second time that week.

Put away wrath, or it will destroy you.

"I made a pan of Lasagna and a salad if anyone's hungry." She headed toward her bedroom. "Just give me a few minutes to freshen up."

"Sounds good, Sis. I'll set the table." Alvin headed to the kitchen, pausing only to look at Gareth. "Preacher man, you up to stay for dinner?"

"I sure am. Lily is with her grandparents for the week, and homemade Lasagna sounds much better than takeout."

Alvin took a plate to Myles's room so that left Gareth alone at the table with Keatyn. Not that he minded. Earlier, Keatyn had caught him off guard while she frolicked on the beach. Watching her in that moment had mesmerized him. He couldn't help but feel an unexpected longing to know her better, especially as he observed her let go of the deep-seated anger that had been holding her captive. The transformation in her demeanor had been striking.

"Alvin tells me you've been with the company where you have worked for over ten years." Gareth brought a fork full of lasagna up to his mouth.

"That's right." Keatyn swallowed down a sip of her tea. "I started there as an intern while still in college."

"What made you decide to attend college in Seattle?" Gareth shoveled in another fork full of lasagna. "This is delicious, by the way."

"Thank you." Keatyn's face heated up with the compliment. "I suppose I wanted a change of scenery." She poured Ranch Dressing on her salad. "That and Washington University gave me a full ride."

"Oh, wow. That makes sense." He cocked his head. "Full scholarship? Can't say that I blame you."

"So, where are you from, Gareth?" Keatyn fidgeted with the moisture coming off her glass.

"My family is from Jacksonville. But Mom's looking to move here soon. We lost my dad last year, and she wants to be near Lily."

"I'm sorry for your loss." Keatyn patted Gareth's hand. "At least Jacksonville's not too far. But I bet it is if you have a grandchild you want to be near."

Tingles shot up Gareth's wrist and arm, which he ignored. "Exactly. Hopefully, we can get her moved soon." Gareth swallowed as he took in how Keatyn rubbed her hand and wrist after touching him. "I offered for her to move in with me, but she declined."

Keatyn took a bite of her salad. "Did you come here just to preach?"

"Not exactly. I started looking for openings when my brother, Jonathan, got stationed here."

"You two must've been close?"

"He and I were best friends, and he was having a hard time." Gareth stared into space and was thankful when Keatyn changed the subject.

"I love my job, but I just want to be back home some days." Keatyn stared outside. Darkness surrounded the beach as the rain continued to drizzle. "You know, living on the beach and working as Captain of my own vessel."

Gareth swallowed his gulp of tea to keep from spewing it in her face. "What did you say? Captain? What kind of vessel?" He got out between coughs.

Keatyn grinned, and her face took on a look of peace. "I would love to open up a business giving tours of our beautiful ocean. I'd take people out to reefs and islands."

Gareth's mouth hung open. "You've surprised me. That's for sure."

Keatyn let out a laugh. "You're not the only one."

After emptying his glass of tea, Gareth rose out of his seat. "Let me help you clean up."

"Nope. You were the guest. I'll clean up." Keatyn cleared the plates off the table. "Besides, it looks like it may blow up soon."

Gareth leaned on the counter. "That wouldn't be fair for me to leave you with all these dishes after cooking such a delicious meal."

Alvin meandered into the room. "No worries, preacher man. I've got cleanup duties."

Gareth nodded, still not feeling right about leaving a mess. "I don't guess I can argue. Thank you so much for dinner."

Keatyn cleared the rest of the table. "Anytime. Have a good night, Gareth."

A boat caught Gareth's eye as he crossed Pensacola Bay bridge. He turned his attention back to the road and pictured what Keatyn would look like in a Captain's hat all the way back to Pensacola. One of the last words she said floated around his mind. *Anytime.*

Chapter 17

Thunder rumbled across the ocean, causing Keatyn to jump out of her skin. Myles gazed at her, and his lips parted in a lopsided grin.

She stood in the kitchen stirring coffee. Even though it was a hot day, the rain made her crave some sweet chocolate goodness. The scent of chocolate and vanilla hijacked the kitchen and caused Keatyn's mouth to water. She leaned down and took in the smell.

The front door crashed open, and her Aunt Tanya rushed in out of the rain. "Y'all." She set her umbrella down. "This storm is not letting up."

"Hey, Aunt Tanya." Keatyn searched the horizon through the open curtains. "The lightning is showing out, and that thunder is loud today."

"Tell me about it." She leaned down and kissed Myles on the forehead before moving to Keatyn.

"Rodney's still in the car on the phone with Vivian. He'll be in shortly."

"Okay." Myles nodded his head.

"How is Vivian doing?" Keatyn asked from the kitchen.

"She's loving college. We don't see her much, but that's to be expected."

"I'm glad she's doing well." Keatyn would've loved college if not for what happened.

She pushed those thoughts away. No good would come from that line of thinking. At least not right now.

"Me, too. I can't wait to see her." Tanya turned her attention to Myles, speaking extra loudly. "You sound better there, big brother. Speech therapy must be working well."

Myles cocked his head. "Yes. Better. Not deaf, though."

"That and his physical therapy is going well. His therapist told me he's making good progress." Keatyn blew on her coffee.

"That's great news. Have you all heard from Alvin?" Tanya shuddered and rubbed down her arms.

"Not Alvin." Myles lowered his gaze.

"He told me not to expect to hear from him for at least a month or more," Keatyn offered.

"Oh. That makes sense. Cordelia put him and his unit in the bulletin, so everyone remembers to pray for their safe return." Tanya wrapped a throw blanket around her shoulders before spearing Keatyn with her gaze. "If you came to service, you'd know."

"That's good to know. And I'll try to come this Sunday." Keatyn placed two mugs of coffee down in front of Tanya. "One for you and one for Uncle Rodney."

"It's a plan." Tanya leaned over and sniffed the mug's contents, wrinkling her nose. "What's in it?"

Keatyn put her hand on her hip. "It's my version of White Chocolate Mocha. Just try it."

Rodney chose that moment to sail into the house. He removed his shoes and rain jacket and shook Myles's hand. "Whew! I couldn't get Vivian off the phone. I finally told her I needed to get inside before I had to swim out of the car."

He took the space beside Keatyn on the sofa and hugged her. "Hi, young'un."

Keatyn hugged him. "Hey, Uncle Rodney." She nodded at the mug. "How's Vivian doing today?"

Tanya clicked her tongue. "Talkative with her dad, that's for sure."

"She loves Arkansas State University." Rodney picked the mug up and drew it to his lips. "Mmm. What's in this?"

Keatyn beamed. "It's a White Chocolate Mocha Latte. Do you like it?"

He blew off some of the steam and took another drink. "Mmmhmm. You may have just converted me to the sweet stuff."

Tanya cleared her throat. "No, sir. You can have one as a special treat on occasion. You're a diabetic, Rodney, so you will stick to your black coffee."

Rodney leaned close to Keatyn and lowered his voice to a whisper. "What she don't know won't hurt her."

Keatyn's abdomen vibrated with a soft laugh. "It'll be our little secret."

Tanya chuckled. "I can hear you two over there plotting."

"Yep, that's what we're doing, Aunt Tanya. Plotting. About coffee."

An explosion of laughter filled the room.

Keatyn took in the smiling faces. Even Myles seemed to be happy. She just wished she could look at him as her dad like she used to.

If only that dreadful day had never happened. If only Mama hadn't wanted french fries so late at night. French fries, of all things. Keatyn had never been able to figure out why.

She was here for one reason. Alvin. And she hoped Myles knew that.

Even though spending time with her family was nice, she accepted that she couldn't stay. Having family was just not meant to be. That way, she would never have to go through that loss again—that debilitating loss.

It was better to be alone.

Chapter 18

A blaring car horn woke Keatyn from a deep sleep way too early. Keatyn rolled over in the bed and squinted at the clock. She groaned. It wasn't even six yet.

Not sure which neighbor had someone honking this early, but she put it on her list to file a complaint. She hopped out of bed and slammed her little toe on the dresser. Sucking in a deep breath, she leaned against the wall. Tears threatened, but she held them back as she put her weight on the uninjured foot.

The front door clicking shut caused the pain to be momentarily forgotten. Keatyn's senses went on high alert, and she cast her eyes around the room for a weapon. She snatched scissors off the dresser and limped out of her bedroom, thankful she'd cut tags off a pair of pants yesterday.

Snores echoed out from underneath Myles's bedroom door. It was up to her to take care of this.

Why didn't she call the police?

She peeked around the hallway and screamed when she came face to face with Aunt Tanya.

The hand holding her weapon of choice dropped to her side. "Are you trying to cause me to have a coronary?"

Tanya puckered her lips out. "Of course not, dummy. I'm here to help you get ready for service."

Frustration lit Keatyn's belly, and she had to swallow it down to keep from saying something she knew she'd regret. Aunt Tanya was only trying to be kind.

Keatyn pushed aside the remark and tried to forget about her throbbing toe. "I appreciate the sentiment, but you know I can get myself ready, Aunt Tanya."

"I know you can." Aunt Tanya's gaze slipped down to the tile. "I just thought it would be nice if I helped you like old times. And I wanted to get here before the home health nurse. So we wouldn't have any distractions."

Keatyn gulped down a steadying breath. "Come on. You can help me pick out my outfit."

Tanya's eyes lit up. "I'm right behind you."

Keatyn held on to Uncle Rodney's arm as they entered the building. Her brow furrowed with regret at the outfit she and Tanya had picked out. She'd wanted to wear a pantsuit, but Tanya talked her into wearing a new flowy white sundress and white Keds.

She'd ridden with her Aunt and Uncle and was glad she had on comfortable shoes in case she needed to make another run for it.

Little butterflies flew around in her stomach. The thought of seeing Kyle happily married was a hard pill to swallow.

Aunt Tanya introduced her to several new people, and then the moment of truth came: Her ex with her old high school friend, Rebecca.

When he walked in with Rebecca, everything made sense. That's why Rebecca said Kyle told her about Keatyn's job.

Wow. That could've been Keatyn. It should've been Keatyn.

Rebecca walked up to her with her arms spread wide. "Oh, Keatyn. I'm so thankful to see you here this morning."

Keatyn's lips turned up into a smile. "It's good to be here." She heard herself say.

Wait. Why was she smiling? She didn't feel a bit weird. Or jealous.

Kyle stuck out his hand. "It's good to see you, Keatyn."

"You, too." She shook his hand and offered up a genuine smile.

The baby in his arms cooed at Keatyn. "Well, aren't you the cutest little thing? What's her name?"

"Her name is Bliss. She's almost a year old and a handful." Rebecca turned her eyes full of love on her daughter.

"Yep, she keeps me on my toes. That's for sure." Kyle replied.

Gareth strolled up to them, and his eyes landed on Keatyn. "Good morning." His lips turned up. "I can't tell you how wonderful seeing you here this morning is."

Keatyn returned his smile, struggling to tear her gaze away from his dimples. Her heart raced, and a knot of conflicting emotions twisted in her stomach.

No. No. No.

This can't happen. She wouldn't allow herself to develop romantic feelings for that man.

No, thank you. She would never. Not ever date a preacher. She'd rather beg Peter to take her back.

Somehow, she kept her composure. "Morning." She smiled at the group and then turned to Aunt Tanya. "We better get settled."

Chapter 19

Keatyn rubbed her hand across the leather binding on Mama's Bible before opening it up.

Taking extra time to rub where JULIE GRIFFIN was imprinted on the corner. The outside of the Bible was worn, but Keatyn would never use another. This was it.

Mama sat in this very building. Holding this very Bible.

Instead of making her sad, peace reverberated throughout her soul. The songs had been uplifting, and Keatyn had a smile on her heart as she focused her attention on the pulpit.

Gareth's voice boomed down from the pulpit. "This morning, our sermon is about our relationship with God."

He clicked a button, and a PowerPoint presentation appeared on the screen behind him. "Brethren, our intention, goal, and desire should be to cultivate a closer relationship with God."

He rustled papers on the podium. "Today, I want to discuss what we must do to deepen our connection with our Father."

Keatyn sat up straighter in her seat and glanced at Aunt Tanya, surprised to see her taking notes.

Gareth continued, "We urgently need that kind of relationship with Him if we want to sustain ourselves daily and navigate life."

Did Keatyn have that kind of relationship with God? If she were honest with herself, she would say no. Bowing her head, she swallowed, her thoughts rampaging.

"This life often besets us with all its troubles, trials, and difficulties. We desperately need to know that we are walking with Him and cultivating a closer relationship.

She had the desire to walk with Him. Didn't she? She did.

"We just sang A Closer Walk With Thee. It's such a beautiful song. And that's what I want each of us to have. A closer walk with God. I pray that each of us enjoys that kind of relationship with our Father."

Keatyn rubbed the back of her neck and focused on her shoes. After a few seconds, she anchored her gaze on Gareth. Even though he was such a natural speaker, she'd missed his last couple of sentences.

Pay attention, Keatyn.

"Because sadly, there are those in this world who do not enjoy their relationship with God."

A couple of verses appeared on the screen. "In fact, you have those who do everything within their power to destroy that relationship. You have those who refuse His grace, love, and direction."

Wait a minute. Had Keatyn done this? Had she tried to destroy her relationship with God?

How many times had she refused His grace?

"Remember what Jesus said in First John 4:19 and 20? Let's read it together."

"We love Him because He first loved us. If someone says, "I love God," and hates his brother, he is a liar; for he who does not love his brother whom he has seen, how can he love God whom he has not seen?"

Keatyn squirmed in her seat. It was a good thing she didn't hate anyone.

What she felt for Myles wasn't hate. She was simply holding him accountable. Actions have consequences. Right?

Gareth's voice echoed as he continued. "But we can't stop there. Read verse 21 with me."

"And this commandment we have from Him: that he who loves God must love his brother also."

Keatyn stepped out of the auditorium, the bright fluorescent lights fading behind her as she entered the dimly lit bathroom. She leaned against the cool marble sink, taking deep breaths to steady herself.

A tingling sensation prickled along her arms, heightening her awareness of the moment.

Had Gareth been talking about her? Or worse, was he speaking directly to her?

The thought felt absurd—how could he know she was attending today? A flicker of suspicion crossed her mind. Perhaps Aunt Tanya had mentioned her.

That must be it. He had tailored his sermon for Keatyn, believing she lacked a genuine connection with God. A wave of frustration washed over her at the idea of being scrutinized that way.

She closed her eyes briefly, grounding herself, before inhaling and exhaling again. After a few moments of reflection, she squared her shoulders and returned to join her family.

Gareth pointed to the screen. "I must be willing to suffer for the cause of Christ. We can look at numerous examples throughout the New Testament of those who gave their lives and suffered for His cause. However, Jesus stands as the best example. He suffered immensely and ultimately gave His life for you and me. His life truly reflects the sacrifice we are called to make. To give our lives and endure suffering for His cause represents a life of sacrifice, a life of service, and a labor of love."

Gareth shifted his gaze across the auditorium, pausing briefly to look at each section before closing his sermon. "Being a disciple of Christ comes with a reward. What is heaven worth to you? Are you seeking that reward? Are you looking for a closer relationship and a deeper walk with God? This morning, you can have it. You can be a Christian like those from the First Century who embraced their faith."

Keatyn no longer listened to Gareth. Pangs beamed through her heart, and she didn't know how to react. There's no way she could let people see her this upset. They won't understand. Or care.

She leaned close to Aunt Tanya. "Hey, I'm going to go to the car. I don't feel well." Grabbing her purse, she didn't give Aunt Tanya a chance to reply before she jumped up and barreled out of the building.

For some reason, she felt that black eyes followed her as she hurried out.

Chapter 20

Keatyn, Myles, and his nurse Jamie sat on the back patio watching the waves hit the shore when a knock sounded from around the front of the house.

"We're back here," Keatyn yelled from the side of the patio.

She arched her eyebrows in disbelief when it was none other than Gareth walking around the house. She glanced down at her baggy pair of capris and old Washington University t-shirt before turning her attention back to the view.

Great. He had some nerve showing up here after that sermon this morning.

Myles clicked the button on his hover round and turned to face Gareth with a big smile. "Hello."

Gareth patted Myles on the shoulder. "Afternoon. You're looking good, Myles. Keep this up, and you'll be back in service in no time."

Myles nodded his head up and down. "Yes."

Gareth cleared his throat. "Um, Keatyn. Can I talk to you for a minute?"

Keatyn avoided eye contact with Gareth. "What is it?"

Myles pointed at the beach. "Take walk."

Jamie chuckled. Probably at the look of panic on Keatyn's face. "Yes, you two take a walk. Myles and I are just fine enjoying the view from here."

Keatyn's heart thumped wildly as she stood up. She shoved the chair underneath the table so hard it screeched in protest. "Let me grab a hat and some more sunscreen."

Gareth leaned down and said something to Myles that Keatyn couldn't make out. She cut her eyes at them before walking up the ramp Alvin had built for Myles before he deployed. Myles pumped his head up and down, and he and Gareth shared a laugh.

Calm down. It's just a walk. On the beach. With him.

After getting the extra sunscreen and hat, Keatyn sashayed down the ramp past Gareth. She turned around and tapped her foot on the sand when he didn't show a sense of urgency.

She let out a long sigh when he still didn't move. "Well, come on. Let's get this over with."

Gareth looked a little guilty as a cringe-laugh escaped his lips. "Yes, ma'am."

Keatyn kicked a log on the trail down to the beach with her bare foot and immediately regretted it.

She'd forgotten about the toe she'd almost knocked off that morning.

Ignoring the throbbing, she turned to Gareth. "What did you want to talk to me about?"

"I had no idea you'd be in service this morning. I was hoping, though." He rubbed his chin and lowered his voice. "I saw the way you left."

Keatyn quickened her pace, and Gareth sped up to keep up with her. A bird hooted in the distance, and her eyes followed it across the sky. Her face softened. If only she could fly anywhere like the bird. How wonderful it would be.

Keatyn gave Gareth a sideways glance. "Maybe I had somewhere to be."

"Did you?"

"Did I what?"

"Have somewhere to be?"

Keatyn stuttered. "Well, technically, yes. I needed to be here."

Gareth tapped the end of his nose. "You tend to say that a lot."

"There are many places I need to be." She walked ahead of Gareth.

He caught up to her quickly. "Listen, I need you to understand I preach to myself first and foremost. If it helps someone else, great. I didn't mean to offend you."

Keatyn took a slow breath through her nose. "Ok. Maybe I did get my feathers ruffled. How could I not?"

He touched her wrist. "That doesn't have to be a bad thing."

His touch caused her to stop in her tracks. "What do you mean by that?"

He turned to Keatyn, his face full of emotion. "It can be a good thing. It's up to you to apply what was said to your life. Or not. No one can force the gospel on you."

Keatyn lifted her shoulders to her earlobes, the long-sleeved cover she'd put over her t-shirt suddenly feeling too heavy. "I guess you're right."

"Truce?" Gareth jutted his hand out at Keatyn.

She eyeballed his hand before grasping it in a weak handshake.

"Come on." He let out a slight laugh. "You can do better than that."

The corners of Keatyn's mouth lifted into a wide grin before she took his hand in a firm shake. "That better?"

"Much." He replied.

The sand shifted, and waves covered their feet. Gareth smiled at Keatyn and splashed her legs with a handful of seawater.

Keatyn gave Gareth a mock, incredulous look. "I see how it is." She kicked at the water, and it sprayed his legs and shirt.

He breathed a hearty laugh, and Keatyn shook her head, laughing with him. She felt free as she laughed with the preacher man, as Alvin called him. It was almost like her teen years. Before their lives, as they knew them, ended.

Chapter 21

Keatyn glanced across the table at Rebecca McDonald. VanHouten. It was Rebecca VanHouten now. She was married to Kyle. "I'm glad you called. I needed a girls' night out."

"Me, too." Rebecca shifted in her chair and crossed her legs, allowing her thin cream pants to pool at her feet. "I was nervous about calling, but Kyle encouraged me, so I did."

"Thank goodness for Kyle." Keatyn intertwined her hands. Her silver glittery shirt sleeve landed at the base of her wrist, and the cold air beating down made her glad to have on a long-sleeved shirt.

After licking her lips, Rebecca gave a half smile. "Yeah."

"I want you to know I'm not holding a grudge or hard feelings if that's what you're worried about. And any feelings I had for Kyle ended when we were teenagers."

Rebecca's shoulders relaxed. "Oh, I know that. I just remembered how you and Kyle were in school and got jealous after seeing you at the hospital."

"Jealous?" Keatyn raised her eyebrows so high she thought they had landed on her head.

"I guess I shouldn't have admitted that, huh?" Rebecca tugged at her earlobe and scanned the restaurant. "It's just that you took my breath away by how beautiful you are now. And I just knew Kyle would regret marrying me after seeing how you turned out. I mean, look at me. I don't look the same as I used to." Her bottom lip quivered.

Old boats, oars, and mounted fish hung all over the walls and ceiling. Keatyn had to admit it was a fascinating design. But Rebecca wasn't admiring the decoration. She was embarrassed.

Time to put on her best reassuring face. Like that one time, she had to lay off several employees, and so many had been nervous and scared. That same face had been her go-too for at least a month. "Rebecca, please listen. You're a beautiful woman. Look at what you've given Kyle. A family. Little Bliss is a dream come true. You have nothing to worry about with me."

Rebecca closed her eyes and laughed nervously. "You must think I'm a nut job."

"Not at all. We all have our moments of doubt. Believe me. I've gone through similar situations myself."

Rebecca's eyes widened. "You have? That's hard to believe. I mean, look at you. You're a Vice President at a major company. You have skin to die for and hair so pretty it should be against the law."

Keatyn anchored her attention on Rebecca. "Beauty is only skin deep. And I'm honestly not that good-looking."

"I'll politely disagree. But I appreciate your words. You've made me feel better, and that means so much to me." Rebecca touched Keatyn's hand.

"Good." Keatyn squeezed the hand Rebecca had put back on the table. "Does this mean we can be friends?"

Rebecca's eyes lit up. "I would love that."

"Awesome." Keatyn scanned the menu. "Now, help me decide what to order. I've been dying to try something new."

Rebecca's phone chose that moment to buzz. She entered her password, and her lips slid into a frown.

Keatyn's brow furrowed. "What's wrong?"

"Bliss is running a high fever. Kyle is taking her to the Emergency Room. Keatyn, I'm sorry, but I need to meet him there."

Concern echoed from Keatyn. "Of course, go. I'll be fine. Promise."

Rebecca stood up as Gareth and Lily walked by their table. "Gareth?"

Gareth spun around and smiled. "Well, hello, ladies."

"Will you please say a prayer for Bliss?" She filled him in on the fever and turned to leave. She paused, her eyes darting from Gareth to Keatyn. "You should invite Keatyn to join you. We haven't even ordered yet."

"Of course. Please text me an update." Gareth turned to Keatyn. "We'd be honored if you'd join us for dinner."

Rebecca waved bye as she rushed out of the restaurant.

Keatyn pulled herself to her feet. "No. I don't want to impose. I'll order mine to go."

"We insist." He nudged Lily. "Don't we, darlin'?"

Her head bobbed up and down. "Pweeease."

Keatyn's face softened as she met Lily's gaze. "How can I say no to such a sweet little girl?"

After settling in, as Gareth watched, Keatyn helped Lily pick out crayons to color her fish. Unfortunately, he wasn't the only one watching them. The man at the next table over kept staring a hole through them.

Keatyn clamped her gaze onto the man until he looked away. Satisfied he got the point, she helped Lily color.

Lily giggled when Keatyn colored a fish pink. "Pretty fisheee."

How easy a life like this could be. The color drained from Keatyn's face as she scolded herself for letting her mind go there. Because this life would never be within her reach. She had everything she could ever need back in Seattle.

Not to mention Keatyn found the way Gareth stared at a gentleman at the other table a bit odd. He almost looked like he'd seen a ghost.

Maybe the man went to church with Gareth, or they'd met somewhere before. They definitely knew one another but didn't seem to want anyone else to know that. Very strange.

Not that any of that mattered. A life such as this would never be hers.

Never.

Chapter 22

The days seemed to fly by on Pensacola Beach. Maybe time passed by quicker for people with less anger in their hearts. Keatyn spent her days working and her evenings getting to know the church members who showed up to help her with Myles.

It was mind-boggling how so many different people offered their assistance. Some helped by sitting with Myles, while others brought meals.

Gareth helped Jamie or Rodney take Myles to his follow-up doctor appointments—every single one of them. And every time he stopped by, Keatyn retreated to the room she'd claimed as an office.

Hopefully, Keatyn would have a day of relaxation away from work for once. Water sprayed her hand as she lowered it beside the boat. Keatyn watched Lily's face and grinned, happy she'd agreed to go on the youth outing with the church.

Memories of the last time she'd been on a boat flashed. She could still picture how Mama's short red hair spiked up from the water. She could hear Mama's contagious laughter as it rang out across the boat. How Mama and Dad had held on to one another as they worked to reel in a Mahi Mahi.

How they playfully argued about who was the better fisherman. Mama would constantly challenge Dad to a "fish off," and it was rare that she lost.

An intense longing entered Keatyn's soul. A need to make her mama proud. She felt that she'd failed at that over the past few years.

Aunt Tanya touched her shoulder. "How are you, dear?"

"I'm fine, Aunt Tanya." She let her eyes settle on a two-story house across the water. "I was just thinking of the last time the family was on a boat together."

Tanya pulled Keatyn close, and Keatyn allowed herself a moment of comfort despite Aunt Tanya's sweaty shirt. "Your mama loved you. So does your dad."

Kyle wandered up to where they stood, followed closely by Rebecca with Bliss on her hip. "Hi, Keatyn. We're so glad you decided to come on our youth outing."

Keatyn gave Rebecca a small smile. "Me, too. It's been nice to see the kiddos enjoy themselves. Takes me back." She pulled the bottom of her t-shirt out.

"And I love this Fort Hill church of Christ Youth Outing t-shirt. I haven't had one of these in a long time."

"Makes me miss my childhood, that's for sure. And yours truly designed our shirts." Bliss thrust her gaze at Rebecca and snatched the sunglasses off her face. "Hey. Give those back."

Keatyn giggled as Bliss fought Rebecca for the sunglasses.

Gareth met Keatyn's eyes from the other side of the boat and grinned. She returned his smile and turned her head. That man caused her to feel things she didn't like.

"Oooh! Look, Dad." Lily pointed at a pod of dolphins swimming beside the boat. She squealed and clapped her hands when they dipped in and out of the water.

Gareth held her tighter to his chest and let out a laugh. "I see them. Aren't they beautiful?"

"Oh, yes, Dad. They are." She turned her head to the side, gazing at Keatyn. "Keatyn. Come see us, pwease."

Keatyn drifted across the boat and stood next to Gareth and Lily. The corners of Gareth's lips quirked into a light smile.

Chill bumps traveled down Keatyn's arms, and she balked. She spun around, and heat traveled up her neck at the knowing look Aunt Tanya had on her face.

Gareth cleared his throat. "Everything all right?"

"Absolutely." She shook her head a little too quickly. "Things are going well. Actually, better than I expected."

Another boat drifted by with passengers eager to see dolphins. A few of them waved. Gareth raised his hand. His spine stiffened and he narrowed his eyes.

Keatyn followed his line of sight and laid eyes on the same man who had been at the restaurant. Now, Keatyn had no doubt Gareth knew him.

Gareth looked away from the other boat. "Myles seems to be happy. I stopped by to see him yesterday, and he said you were working. Again." Gareth propped his leg on the rail.

Keatyn rolled her shoulders and gasped when a dolphin swam by. "Yes, I'm still working remotely."

"Will you be at service Sunday? I know Myles would love to come."

Her answer was a clipped, "I plan on it."

"Have I done something else to offend you?" He searched her gaze for answers.

Keatyn nipped at the inside of her bottom lip. "Why would you ask that?"

"You seem distant. So I was wondering –"

"Not at all." Keatyn paused and closed her eyes. "Honestly, I can't shake the feeling that you knew the man at the restaurant but didn't want anyone to find out. I just saw him again on that boat."

"In that case," Gareth said, swallowing hard, "would you be interested in going for another walk on the beach sometime soon? We can talk about it."

A wave of excitement surged through Keatyn. "I'm looking forward to it." She wanted to know who the man was. Nothing more.

An amused expression appeared on Gareth's face as he raised an eyebrow. "That's good to know."

Keatyn's eyes widened in surprise. "That didn't come out right."

"If you say so," Gareth replied with a smirk.

"I think Aunt Tanya is feeling lonely." She leaned down to hug Lily. "I'll see you all later." Turning back to Gareth, she added, "Call me when you're ready for that walk."

Later that night, Jamie, the home health nurse, helped Myles settle into bed when Keatyn walked by.

"Keatyn?"

She stopped in her tracks and poked her head around the door. "What's up?"

"Will you come in here, please?" His speech sounded better and better.

Maybe she would get to go home soon. She stepped inside the room and walked close to his bed. Myles waited until Jamie said her goodbyes before he met Keatyn's gaze.

"Please tell me you've forgiven me." Tears pooled in the rims of his eyes.

Put away wrath.

Mama's words settled in her mind.

Does putting away wrath mean she had to forgive?

She opened her mouth and closed it.

Myles put his hand out. "Don't answer me yet. I can wait. You being here is enough."

Keatyn managed to nod her head. Her tightened, and she struggled to catch her breath until she reached her bedroom.

Chapter 23

Rodney helped Myles into his wheelchair and then pushed him through the double doors of the church. After Bible class and singing, they settled in for the sermon. Keatyn noticed the joy on Myles's face, and a tinge of guilt washed over her.

Maybe she should have brought him to church sooner. He looked so happy here, though she tried to convince herself that she didn't care about his happiness. Why should she?

Put away wrath.

No matter how hard she tried, she couldn't stop Mama's words from echoing in her mind. She knew she needed to let go of her anger, but that was much easier said than done. As she looked up, Gareth began his sermon.

He clicked a button, and the PowerPoint screen displayed a picture of chains. "While Paul was imprisoned in chains in Rome, he authored the book of Philippians. We all know he could have chosen to wallow in self-pity and complaints. However, he refrained from doing so."

A few Bible verses appeared on the screen. "Rather than becoming self-centered or overly worried, Paul understood that this was not his mission. Instead, he dedicated his time to encouraging others. Turn with me to Philippians chapter 4, verses 4 through 7."

"Rejoice in the Lord always. Again I will say, rejoice! Let your gentleness be known to all men. The Lord is at hand. Be anxious for nothing, but in everything by prayer and supplication, with thanksgiving, let your requests be made known to God; and the peace of God, which surpasses all understanding, will guard your hearts and minds through Christ Jesus."

He clicked on the next slide, which displayed pictures of shackles and bullet points. "You and I may not be physically bound, but many of us wear shackles of different sizes and lengths. They could be the result of failing health or a serious medical issue. Perhaps they stem from an unhappy marriage, difficult relationships, or children who break our hearts. It might also be related to job stress or financial struggles."

Keatyn's mind focused on the part about children breaking hearts. What about parents?

Gareth stepped back from the podium and raised his voice. "We all find ourselves, in one way or another, shackled by the wages of sin, the trials and difficulties of this life. Chains that can cause us to be dissatisfied, unhappy, depressed, and occasionally discouraged or sad."

Gareth's eyes rested on each section before moving to the next slide. "So, how do we escape? How do we turn the tables on Satan and the world? How could the apostle Paul be happy in his chains? And how can we be happy in ours? The answer is found in Philippians."

Gareth flipped a few pages back in his Bible. "First of all, we should look at the past with thanksgiving to God. Let's read Philippians 1 verses 3 through 5."

"I thank my God upon every remembrance of you, Always in every prayer of mine for you all making request with joy, For your fellowship in the gospel from the first day until now."

"Paul was happy in chains because he looked at the past with thanksgiving. He looked for the good in all things."

Keatyn tapped her toes. A tinge of shame for her earlier thoughts traveled up her spine. She inspected her freshly manicured fingernails, willing to look at anything to keep from meeting those eyes. Lately, she had been getting embarrassed by her line of thoughts. Maybe that meant she needed to change her way of thinking.

Gareth's voice seemed to command her attention. "It's incredible that Paul did not look back with malice or hatred at his maltreatment. So often, those who have been wronged or perceive they've been wronged are quick to relive it and show malice, contempt, and hatred. But not Paul. Can you imagine? Mad at a man and taking it out on God? Some do! But Paul didn't, and we need to take a lesson. Perhaps, when he reflected on the unpleasant events, he saw the good that came from them."

Gareth flipped through his Bible again. "Like what Paul told the Romans in chapter 8, verse 28, we may not understand why a certain thing happens. It may be Satan trying to destroy your faith or trying to get you to destroy the faith of others. He may be trying to cause persecution to overwhelm you. To cause you to cast off God, give up, give in, get mad, deny the faith, and leave the church."

Had Satan done this to Keatyn? How was she supposed to know?

It was like Gareth could read her mind. "We may not understand a lot of things. But one thing is for sure: God will be there for us to help us in times of need. Paul looked for the good and focused on good memories."

Did Keatyn have good memories to focus on?

Of course.

Mama made sure Keatyn had the best childhood she could give me.

And Dad did, too.

Until he forsook Mama.

But did he really forsake her?

"Paul could be happy in chains because he remembered the past with thanksgiving to God. You and I can concentrate on the bad things that happen in our lives and end up bitter, or like Paul, we can remember the good things, give thanks to the Lord, rejoice, and be happy. Happiness is the result of a joyful heart. Happiness is a choice."

Wow. Here, Keatyn sat, focusing on the bad things that had happened. Maybe she'd lived for years focusing on the bad. Shouldn't she focus on the good things instead?

Happiness is a choice.

Those four words circled in Keatyn's mind.

She'd made her own choices. Could it be she'd caused her bitterness?

Would Mama be proud of her?

Her stomach flipped, and she couldn't sit still. Her mind drifted to happier days. After a few minutes, she'd missed a good part of the sermon. She took a few deep breaths, focused on breathing, and listened to Gareth.

"What will your reaction be to the chains of life? Like Paul, let us look to them with thanksgiving. Let us look at the chains of life with confidence in God. Knowing that He is there, fighting for us and standing with us. Looking at the future with prayer. Relying on the strength of the Lord. Tell me, where are your eyes fastened? Do you truly desire a home in heaven? Then what are you waiting for? You can become a Christian just like those in the first Century became Christians. It's a cookie-cutter process!"

Maybe it's time for Keatyn to put her whole heart into studying.

Chapter 24

Keatyn moved her small carry-on bag from one shoulder to another as she boarded a small plane at the Destin - Fort Walton Beach Airport.

She'd left before taking that walk with Gareth. He'd called a few times, but she kept putting him off. Her mind had been a pool of confusion since his last sermon. She was uncertain about the path she needed to take for the first time in a long while.

Other women her age were married. Many had families. Happiness. But Keatyn? She had a job to keep her warm at night. And that was it. True love had eluded her.

She caught a glimpse of her green cargo pants and almost laughed out loud. She hadn't dressed so casually in a very long time. It felt good. Different, but not in a bad way.

Aunt Tanya and Uncle Rodney had agreed to stay with Myles for a few days so Keatyn could attend the annual upper leadership meeting at Westfield Financial.

She planned to finish things quickly and return home before the week was out.

Home?

Did she really think of Pensacola Beach as home?

When did that happen?

A pair of black eyes and dimples swam around her mind, and she silently sighed, feeling the weight of unwanted desires.

It had nothing to do with that man.

Liar.

It did have something to do with him, she admitted.

Keatyn forced her mind to think about something else. Like Myles. Not her favorite subject, but one that could no longer be avoided.

Myles needed someone there with him all the time. And really, there was no one else. Alvin's deployment got extended for three more months at the least, so Keatyn had to step up, as Alvin had not so nicely put it.

What next? Maybe she should stop trying to analyze everything and take it a day at a time.

The plane shook as it hit turbulence, and Keatyn smiled at the woman beside her. She held a Bible in her lap and, after returning Keatyn's smile, closed her eyes and mouthed what sounded like a prayer.

"I'm deathly afraid to fly." The woman finally announced.

"I don't love it, but I don't get too scared. Unless we hit hard turbulence." Keatyn glanced out the window. Moisture hit her eyes as they landed on a stack of fluffy clouds. "I do love the view, though."

The woman let out a sigh. "My daughter is pregnant and could give birth any day now. She'd never forgive me if I'm not there when the baby's born."

"I understand." Keatyn popped a piece of gum in her mouth. She tried to hand the woman the package, but she declined.

"I wouldn't be here without prayer. That's for sure. Even though I'm afraid to fly, I trust God will keep me safe." She held her Bible to her chest.

A smile breezed over Keatyn's lips. "That's good."

Keatyn picked up a magazine and flipped through the pages, assuming the conversation had ended.

The woman's lip twitched. "My doctor gave me something for my nerves, but I hate taking pills."

"Same. I have a hard time even taking a Tylenol." Keatyn raised her brows.

"My name is Wendy," she said, offering Keatyn a shaky hand. "What's your name?"

Keatyn shook her hand. "Nice to meet you. I'm Keatyn."

Wendy clenched her fists. "Do you often fly, Keatyn?"

Keatyn kept her tone calm as she spoke to Wendy. "I've flown a handful of times for work and several times for personal travel."

Wendy turned hopeful eyes on Keatyn. "And nothing bad's ever happened to you?"

"Not flying, at least." Keatyn sighed.

Wendy leaned closer to Keatyn. "Uh oh. Do you want to talk about it with a stranger? It may make you feel better."

Keatyn almost told her no, but her kind smile broke through Keatyn's hardened heart.

Why not?

It's not like they'd ever see one another again.

Keatyn opened her mouth and shared her life story with Wendy.

Wendy patted her hand several times as Keatyn relived her gripping past.

Even though Keatyn left out the part about how Gareth caused her heart to flutter, Wendy seemed to know. Keatyn's face softened when she told her about their first meeting.

Keatyn took in a long breath and met Wendy's soft gaze. "So, that's my life in a nutshell. I'm alone, and that's the way I like it."

Wendy rubbed her chin. "Dear Keatyn, I perceive you have suffered many hardships and have allowed them to take over your heart."

Keatyn opened her mouth to protest but decided against it. She squeezed her eyes shut as if in physical pain.

Wendy scratched her arm. "God never promised that our lives would be a bowl of cherries. Instead, He said we'd never have more than we can handle."

"Mama always said God would help us when we have more than we can take. But lately, I've felt like

I have way more than I can handle, and there's no one there to help. Especially not God."

Wendy's voice came out low and steady. "Of course, that's what I meant. If we rely on God, He will help us through our struggles."

Keatyn held back the tears. Only weak people openly cried. "Losing Mama changed my life."

"Losing one's parents always changes our life. But it's up to us to determine *how* it changes our life," Wendy replied, leaning closer.

Keatyn furrowed her brow. "What do you mean by that?"

"I mean, we can live a life full of bitterness and hatred or determine that we'll be happy even in our hardships." Wendy leaned closer to Keatyn. "Would your mama want you to be so bitter?"

"You sound like Gareth," Keatyn snapped, clicking her tongue.

Wendy's lips turned up at the corners. "I don't know this, Gareth, but based on what you've told me, I'll take that as a compliment anyway."

Before they knew it, the Pilot's voice echoed over the speaker, notifying them they would be landing soon.

"Thank you for taking the time to talk to me, Keatyn. You helped calm my nerves. And I'll keep you and your family in my prayers." Wendy squeezed Keatyn's hand. "Think about what I said. I think your mama would want you to be happy. To truly embrace happiness."

"Thank you for listening. And for the advice." Keatyn grinned at Wendy. "And I wish you and your family the best in life."

A little later, Keatyn stood at the curb, waiting for her ride. A significant weight had been lifted from her shoulders. The conversation with Wendy had been a blessing, bringing a sense of relief.

She pulled up social media to pass the time. The first post took her breath away.

Lucy Parnell and Peter Brockton announce their engagement.

Chapter 25

Keatyn stepped off the back patio and entered the kitchen. Though she wouldn't admit it to Myles, she was excited to be back at Pensacola Beach.

The meeting with the executives had gone very well. Jean Cordell, the CEO of Westfield Financial, offered Keatyn a position in the Gulf States. Their current Vice President, Kade Monroe, would transfer to London in two months.

Jean gave Keatyn four weeks to decide. After that, he'd have to go with his second choice.

No pressure.

Pensacola Beach had always been and continued to be her happy place. But Seattle had become her home. Still, she hadn't felt so free in years.

It had to be the ocean and the white sand.

She glanced over at the table and shook her head. She'd never heard of grown adults playing Go Fish. It was hilarious.

Cordelia Inman glanced down at her cards and smirked at Dad. "Go fish, sucker!"

Dad let out a laugh. "That's no way to talk, Del."

"Yes, it is when you're the undefeated winner," Cordelia said, covering her mouth with the back of her hand as if trying to stifle a giggle. She reminded Keatyn of a schoolgirl with a crush.

Dad threw his cards on the table. "I still think you cheat."

The humorous quips between them brought a sense of light-heartedness to the room. Keatyn leaned against the kitchen counter, watching the two banter back and forth. Dad put on a good show, but the twinkle in his eye told Keatyn he was teasing Cordelia.

Four months had passed since his stroke, and he had made excellent progress with his speech and mobility. Keatyn would have already moved back to Seattle, but Alvin was still away, and Dad wasn't ready to live independently. Or perhaps he was, but Keatyn didn't want to admit it. She tried not to dwell on it too much.

Cordelia had come over every afternoon after she finished at the church. She had been a tremendous help to Keatyn, and she made Dad smile.

If Keatyn didn't know better, she'd swear Dad had feelings for Cordelia. But Alvin said Dad hadn't so much as looked at another woman after Mama passed.

That doesn't mean he wouldn't. And if Dad wanted to date another woman, Keatyn would be okay with it. Especially if the woman happened to be Cordelia. She was five years his senior, but that didn't matter. Cordelia was a good woman. Kind. A woman Keatyn would be proud to call stepmother.

She took a seat at the table, a glint touching her eyes. "I take it Cordelia's tearing you a new one again."

Dad let out a hmph. "I let her win."

Cordelia gawked at Myles. "You just accused me of cheating. Now you claim that you let me win? I think you need to get your story straight, Mr. Griffin."

A rash of warmth stained Dad's neck and ears. "Well, it has to be one of the two options. Cause I'm good at playing goldfish."

A burst of giggles stirred in Keatyn's stomach, and she choked them down. Goldfish?

Oh my. He's turning red. She must be right.

A knock at the door interrupted Keatyn's thoughts. "Excuse me."

Keatyn opened the door to find Gareth on the other side. She stepped aside. "Come on in."

Gareth strode forward with a grin. "I didn't know you were back."

"Yeah, I just got back last night."

His eyes sparkled as he took the empty seat beside Dad. "I would've been happy to pick you up at the airport," he said.

Keatyn's eyes flew to his. "I drove Dad's truck there and parked it at the airport. But I appreciate you."

Cordelia stood up. "The two of you may as well join us for a game of dominoes. Myles is tired of me beating him at Go Fish." She peeked around Gareth. "And just where is my Lily?"

"She's at a sleepover with her cousin. You know that girl is a social butterfly."

Cordelia pinned Gareth with her eyes. "She needs a mother in her life."

Gareth let out a nervous laugh, then nudged Keatyn. "Wanna partner up against those two? I think we can win."

Keatyn clapped her hands together. "Oh, yes. I know we can. But first, I'll make coffee."

Dad met Keatyn's gaze, and the corners of his mouth curled upwards into a wide grin. "You called me Dad."

Her lips twitched until a small smile cracked the edges of her mouth. "I guess I did."

Chapter 26

Keatyn's eyelids fluttered open to the sound of her phone ringing. She lifted her head slightly before plopping it back down on the pillow. When the ringing stopped, she rolled over and threw one leg out of bed. It wasn't quite daylight yet, and she wasn't interested in waking up this early. Just as she settled back in, the phone began ringing again.

"Okay." She said to the empty bedroom. She leaned over and checked the caller ID. A private number flashed across the screen.

Her lungs tightened as she pressed the green button. "Alvin? Is that you?"

Static crackled on the other end as the caller struggled to be heard over the noise. Finally, she discerned one word: "Sis."

"What's wrong?" she shouted into the phone.

"Can you hear me?" Alvin's voice came through louder now. "I had to adjust things for a better signal."

"Yes, I can hear you. What has happened?"

"Please forgive me."

She sat up abruptly on the side of the bed. "Forgive you for what?"

"Sis, I almost died. I can't give you the details, but my leg is messed up. I'm in the infirmary and probably going to be sent home."

"Oh, Alvin. Are you sure you're okay?" She grabbed a tissue and wiped her nose. "You don't need my forgiveness for that."

"No. Not that." The sound of Alvin weeping made Keatyn's heart flip in her chest.

"Mama dying was my fault."

"What do you mean?" Keatyn's face paled, and she clutched her throat.

"I'm so sorry. I've never told you the truth."

Part of the conversation she overheard at the hospital replayed in her mind. "Tell me now." Keatyn pressed her lips together, forming a thin line.

Alvin sobbed, "Mama was making those French fries for me, Keatyn." A heavy silence fell on the other end of the line, causing concern to course through her veins.

"Alvin?" Keatyn shrieked. "Bubba? Talk to me."

"I had my headphones on playing my video game and didn't hear the fire alarm in time to save her." Alvin cried out between sobs. "It's my fault."

Her breath hitched in her throat. "What?"

"I'm so sorry. After you rushed back to college and refused to speak to Dad, I feared you'd want nothing to do with me."

Bile rose from her stomach, settling in her throat. "I don't blame you. I wish you'd told me sooner, but I don't blame you. You were just a kid." She clutched her fuzzy blanket to her throat.

"So you'll be there when I get home?"

"Yes, I'll be here."

"Do you promise you don't hate me?"

"I promise I don't hate you."

"Sis?"

"Mmmhmm?"

"Will you ask Gareth to pray extra for my team to make it home?"

"Of course I will, Alvin. Please stay safe."

"I love you, Keatyn. And I really am sorry."

"I love you, too, Bubba. Don't give it another thought. See you soon."

Keatyn hung up the phone and buried her face in her pillow. For the first time in many years, she cried sorrowfully for someone else.

Chapter 27

Sweat beaded across Keatyn's brow as she jogged along the shore. Scenarios of her future as a wife and mother played in her mind. She picked up her pace and focused on Alvin and the blame he must've carried all those years.

She hated that he kept the truth from her. But could she blame him? Not after the way she acted. Mama would never blame Alvin, and she would be mad if Keatyn did. It's not like he left her to die. That was on someone else. Those thoughts battered her insides to the point she pushed them far away.

Gareth and Rodney were already on the way to pick Alvin up from the airport this morning in the church van so he would have plenty of room to prop his leg up. But what should Keatyn do next? The plan had always been for her to go straight back to Seattle when Alvin got home. But now, he was in no condition to care for Dad. Not with an injury of his own to deal with.

As she slowed to a walk, she played around with different scenarios in her mind.

At first, she daydreamed about eventually returning to Seattle and continuing as the Vice President of Westfield Financial.

Things were great for a while.

But she was alone.

Forever.

She kicked her speed up as another thought came to her. She could move to Pensacola Beach permanently. She'd find a cute little bungalow right on the beach and be the Gulf States Vice President.

But she was alone.

Forever.

Why do all scenarios in her head end up with her being alone? Maybe that's the way she liked it. No, being alone isn't fun. She had wanted things to work out with Peter.

She had. They just weren't right for each other. He'd been spot-on about that.

What about Gareth?

That wasn't even worth dreaming about. Even if she wanted to, he'd never marry someone like Keatyn. Seattle would be her best bet. Surely, she'd find someone eventually.

Gareth's deep laugh invaded her thoughts, but she forced it out by focusing on the waves crashing into the shore.

She slowed down and walked a few seconds before stopping and leaning her hands on her legs. She had half a mile left before she'd be back home.

Rebecca had called to invite her for a girl's night out earlier. And Keatyn found that she was looking forward to it. They'd been the best of friends in high school, and the fact that Rebecca married Keatyn's high school sweetheart didn't bother her as much as she thought it would, a fact that still shocked Keatyn.

Keatyn figured she'd have time for a reunion with Alvin before leaving. From what Dad had told her, Alvin would want his space for a little bit. At least he had the last time he returned from a deployment.

The ache in her chest was a stark reminder of the days when stress had almost overwhelmed her. But this time, it wasn't just stress. She was burdened with too many regrets over how she had handled things over the past ten years. Her heart ached, especially for not spending more time with her brother. What if he had been killed over there?

An orange and cream shell caught her eye, and she picked it up. She turned it over in her hand and grinned. It was perfect. Vibrant and whole.

She took a swig of her water before continuing on her hunt. She found a few more shells and a shark tooth before returning home. She picked up her pace as soon as the beach house appeared.

She entered the back of the house, glancing into Dad's room as she strolled by. She froze in place, taking in the scene before her. He had his back to the door as he pulled a loose shirt on.

"What's on your back?" Her voice started low but ended up high-pitched.

Dad slowly turned and met her eyes. He paused a few seconds, setting his mouth into a firm line. "Burn scars."

"From what?"

A voice came from the living room. "From pulling Mama out of that fire."

Keatyn whipped her head around towards the living room. She squealed and torpedoed across the room. "Bubba!"

Alvin opened his arms as Keatyn lowered herself beside him on the sofa. "It's good to see you, Sis."

She pressed her head into his side and exhaled a long puff of air. "You, too."

Rodney cleared his throat. "Can we get you anything before we drop the van off at the building?"

"Nah, I'm good. Thank you both for picking me up."

"You're welcome," Gareth said. "Call me if you need me. Lily is back at her grandma's visiting with her cousins, so I can be here whenever."

"Thank you, preacher man. That means a lot to me."

Keatyn kept her face firmly planted in her brother's side, never once looking up. She barely managed to huff out a goodbye to Gareth and Rodney.

Chapter 28

A few days later, Cordelia stuck her head inside Gareth's office. "Guess who just pulled up?"

The corners of Gareth's lips tugged into a smile as he cocked his head. "Well, I'm not sure. I don't have an appointment, so I'd assume one of the church members?"

"Nope." For some reason, Cordelia grinned from ear to ear. "It's Keatyn."

Gareth's heart thudded in his chest. He vigorously shook his head as if trying to shake off the very notion of romance. He knew better than to allow his feelings to get out of control.

"Good deal." Gareth clutched the collar of his light pink button-up. "I know you were planning to leave and grab some office supplies, but will you do me a favor and stick around?"

Cordelia put her hand on her hip. "Now you know you don't even have to ask."

Gareth's shoulders relaxed. "Thank you."

A few minutes later, Keatyn pecked on Gareth's door. "Do you have a few minutes?"

Gareth shot up out of his chair. "I sure do. What's up?"

She fiddled with the tie on the front of her dark green dress. "Well, I was wondering if you would help me understand what Matthew 18:35 means."

A smile flashed across Gareth's face. "Absolutely." He opened the Bible on his desk and read the verse aloud.

"So My heavenly Father also will do to you if each of you, from his heart, does not forgive his brother his trespasses."

"To get the full context, we need to read the full passage. Let's start at verse 21 and read through 35."

"Then Peter came to Him and said, "Lord, how often shall my brother sin against me, and I forgive him? Up to seven times?" "Jesus said to him, "I do not say to you, up to seven times, but up to seventy times seven."

Keatyn scrunched up her lips. "Wait a minute. Is this saying we have to forgive someone four hundred and ninety times? How are we supposed to keep count?"

Gareth shook his head. "This isn't a literal number. Jesus explains to Peter here that we should forgive as often as someone truly seeks our forgiveness."

"Okay. That makes sense. Please continue."

"Therefore the kingdom of heaven is like a certain king who wanted to settle accounts with his servants. And when he had begun to settle accounts, one was brought to him who owed him ten thousand talents. But as he was not able to pay, his master commanded that he be sold, with his wife and children and all that he had, and that payment be made. The servant therefore fell down before him, saying, 'Master, have patience with me, and I will pay you all.' Then the master of that servant was moved with compassion, released him, and forgave him the debt."

Keatyn cleared her throat, prompting Gareth to stop reading. "Do you have another question?"

She ran her hands through her hair and fixed her unblinking gaze on Gareth. "How are we supposed to know if someone is truly sorry?"

"If someone has wronged you and comes to you humbly asking for forgiveness, why would you judge their heart?"

Keatyn glanced down at the text before looking back at Gareth. "Well, I suppose I shouldn't judge their heart. Shouldn't I leave that to God?"

Gareth smiled and nodded before continuing to read.

"But that servant went out and found one of his fellow servants who owed him a hundred denarii; and he laid hands on him and took him by the throat, saying, 'Pay me what you owe!' So his fellow servant fell down at his feet and begged him, saying, 'Have patience with me, and I will pay you all.' And he would not, but went and threw him into prison till he should pay the debt."

Keatyn licked her lips and held up her hand. "Wait a minute. Are you saying the same man who had his debt forgiven refused to forgive another?"

He pointed to the verse, a small smile lifting his lips. "I'm not saying anything. I'm reading what happened."

She raised her left brow and leaned her elbow on the desk. "Okay, smartie pants. That's how I understand it. Am I wrong?"

"Not according to my studies."

Keatyn twisted her earring back and forth. "Okay, will you please read the rest?"

"So when his fellow servants saw what had been done, they were very grieved and came and told their master all that had been done. Then his master, after he had called him, said to him, 'You wicked servant! I forgave you all that debt because you begged me. Should you not also have had compassion on your fellow servant, just as I had pity on you?' And his master was angry, and delivered him to the torturers until he should pay all that was due to him. So My heavenly Father also

will do to you if each of you, from his heart, does not forgive his brother his trespasses."

She had a blank expression on her face. One that told Gareth she was deep in thought.

"Do we expect God to forgive our debts?" Gareth's normal loud voice was almost muted as he tried to express his thoughts. "When we ask, God forgives our debts, does He not?"

Keatyn nodded her head in agreement.

"Yet, how quickly you and I sometimes forget to offer the same mercy to others. Often, when we perceive a wrong, we are so upset that we reject their pleas of sorrow."

Keatyn's voice came out in a whisper. "The man was delivered to the tormentors. Why?"

"Because he was so hard-hearted, he didn't offer the same compassion that was offered to him. He refused to forgive. And there were consequences."

"So, you're saying I have to forgive." Keatyn's blue eyes flashed. "No matter what. Someone can kill a family member, but I don't have the right to hold them responsible?"

"God is saying when the person who wronged us realizes and approaches us with a spirit of true repentance, then we should and must be ready to forgive them."

Keatyn's lips twitched downward. Gareth briefly touched her hand. "Do you truly blame Myles for your mother's death? Do you think he killed her?"

After looking out the window for a few seconds, it came out in a very slight whisper when she spoke. "No."

Gareth continued, "Let's look at what Paul wrote to the brethren at Ephesus in Ephesians 4:32."

"And be kind to one another, tenderhearted, forgiving one another, just as God in Christ forgave you."

"I guess I've never looked at it like that. I've been so angry."

"Holding things in your heart destroys your peace, happiness, and well-being. God knew that holding things in our hearts could cause us problems. That's why the command to forgive was given."

She shifted in her seat and crossed her legs. "Maybe my hatred has caused many problems."

"You lost your mother, which was a tragedy. But to forgive, you have to give up that hatred you've been holding on to."

"What if I don't know how?" Keatyn turned distressed eyes to Gareth. "Losing my mom damaged me, Gareth."

"You didn't just lose one parent. You lost both." Gareth's soothing voice seemed to dampen her distress.

Keatyn blinked a few times. "You're right. How can I change the way I feel?"

"Hate and loss and separation are tools of the devil. Reconciliation, love, and unity are tools of God. Allow God into your life. Into your heart."

Her forehead creased, and she flattened her lips. "What do I do about Myles?"

"Your dad doesn't know what to do to get the relationship with you back. He knows it's up to you. Have you considered forgiving him?"

"I have. But maybe I can't handle that right now. What if it's too much?"

"God doesn't put more on you than you can handle, with His help. Have you ever considered that you don't have to walk through this life alone? God will be with you, but you have to let Him."

Tears brimmed in the corners of her eyes. "I've pushed everyone away, including God."

"Keatyn, I know you're a strong woman. And you have a good heart – even though you try to hide it."

A sudden lightness appeared on Keatyn's face, and she raised herself to her feet. "Thank you for taking the time to study with me. Even though I didn't have an appointment."

"My door is always open. No appointment needed."

"Thanks again. I think I know what I need to do." She paused and cocked her head". Maybe you can tell me how you know the man from the restaurant and boat next time we talk." With that, she inched towards the door and strode out of his office.

Chapter 29

Wrath. Extreme anger. Rage. Keatyn winced as those words echoed in her mind. That's what she had lived with for the past ten years. Who was she kidding? She hadn't just lived with those feelings; she had embraced them.

With turmoil swirling inside her, she barely made it through the yellow light before it turned red beside the Shrimp Shack. Her mouth watered at the thought of a plate of shrimp, and she would have stopped for a quick bite if she weren't on a mission.

As she continued down the road, warm air carried the sound of laughter from a local art studio.

Keatyn shifted nervously in her seat, quickly slamming on the brakes when a couple stepped out in front of her. In Florida, pedestrians had the right of way.

"Sorry!" she called out the window, earning a glare from the woman.

Biting back a snide remark, she rolled the window up. By the time she parked, her heart was racing. To calm herself, she laid her head on the steering wheel.

She needed to quit putting it off. Wasn't it time for her to step up and make Mama proud?

Whisking through the open door, she found Jamie, Myles, Cordelia, and Alvin watching some home improvement show about a beach house flip.

Keatyn cleared her throat. "Hey."

Alvin's face lit up. "Hey, Sis."

Keatyn clutched her Coach purse tight. "Hey. Can we talk for a minute?"

Alvin pointed at Myles, and Keatyn couldn't help but grin. A small pool of drool had landed on his shirt. He was sound asleep.

Myles opened one eye and then the other. He rubbed the sleep from his eyes with one hand and wiped his chin. He smiled from ear to ear at Keatyn. "Making fun of me, huh?"

Keatyn covered her mouth and widened her eyes. "Never."

"Do either of you need something to drink or snack on?" Keatyn looked at the kitchen.

Quit putting off the talk. Chicken.

"I'll take some ice water," Myles answered.

Jamie got to her feet. "I can get it."

Keatyn paused. "All right. But after that, would you take a break for an hour or so?"

Jamie shrugged. "Sure thing. I actually have some errands to run."

Cordelia raised herself out of her seat. "I better head out as well."

Keatyn grasped Cordelia's hand. "Thank you."

Myles seemed to hesitate before asking, "Is everything okay?"

Keatyn took the empty recliner and straightened her top. "Of course."

Myles closed his eyes and laid his head back.

Jamie's Toyota Highlander engine gunned to life as she backed out of the driveway with Cordelia close behind in her Cadillac.

With trembling hands, Keatyn tucked her hair behind her ear. "I don't know where to start. So, I'll start with a question." She swallowed and took a deep breath. "Will you both please forgive me?"

Myles leaned his head back for a split second, relief oozing from his features. "Oh, baby girl." He pulled himself to his feet and walked towards Keatyn, arms open wide. "I just said a silent prayer that you weren't telling us you'd be going back to Seattle."

Keatyn sprung to her feet and threw herself in his arms. "I'm so sorry, Dad!" She got out between sobs. "I've been so selfish."

"It's all right." Tears streamed down his face. "Everything is going to be just fine."

She turned to Alvin. "What about you?"

Alvin nodded and wiped the moisture away from his cheeks. "Yes, I forgive you. Always. Now get down here and give me a hug."

They joined Alvin on the couch and entwined their hands.

Keatyn pulled out a tissue and blew her nose. "There's so much I feel I need to say. I know I need to make amends. I just have to figure out how."

Myles squeezed her hand. "It's forgotten. We forgive you, and that's all we need to say about it. Let's start today by focusing on being a family."

Alvin shook his head up and down. "I agree with Dad. You asking forgiveness is an answer to our prayers, Sis. I vote we start fresh and do our best to bring glory and honor to God for answering our prayers."

"Thank you. I love y'all," Keatyn whispered.

"And we love you. So very much." Dad echoed back at her.

After a few minutes, Keatyn sat up and eyeballed Dad. The corners of her mouth gave a whisk of a smile. "I'm glad you're finally sharing that you're doing better with us."

Dad flinched and met her gaze. "So, you knew?"

"Well, yeah. I saw you walking a few weeks ago." She picked at her fingernail. "And I've noticed you trying to sway your speech on purpose."

Dad fell silent for a minute before he flashed a grin at her. "And you didn't leave? You're not angry with me?"

Keatyn raised a brow. "I think there's been enough anger in this family to last a lifetime. Wouldn't you both agree?"

"Yes." Dad and Alvin answered in unison.

"Will you forgive me for misleading you?"

"It's forgotten." Keatyn said, picking up her iPhone, a look of determination crossing her face." I'm calling Aunt Tanya and Uncle Rodney to get them over here. I have to make things right with them as well."

Chapter 30

No matter how hard he tried to focus on other things, Gareth found himself trapped by thoughts of the woman who'd recently left his office.

Keatyn Griffin's vibrant, turquoise blue eyes sparkling with mischief, and her captivating smile could light up even the darkest days. Even though she had her struggles, everyone around her seemed to be drawn in by her infectious energy, their troubles momentarily forgotten in her presence.

As he recalled her laughter, warmth surged within him, and for a fleeting moment, he couldn't deny the magnetic pull of attraction. His jaw tightened at the realization.

The last thing he wanted was to entangle himself with her emotions or risk getting hurt. Falling for her would be a gamble he had no desire to take, and yet, her image lingered in his mind, tempting him to reconsider. No, he couldn't. That was a risk he wasn't willing to take, thank you very much.

Even if he were foolish enough to entertain those feelings, he couldn't help but wonder if someone like her could ever be genuinely interested in a preacher. The odds seemed impossible, and he couldn't shake the feeling that their worlds were too different.

He took a deep breath, reminding himself to stay focused on the path before him, which required his full attention and devotion.

Cordelia poked her head inside his office. "I'm heading out," she said before quickly moving down the hall.

Gareth pulled himself out of his chair and walked to the hallway. "Have a good afternoon."

"I plan on it." Her cheeks reddened, reminding Gareth of the apple he'd snacked on earlier.

His lips quivered into a smile. "Tell Myles hello from me."

Cordelia's head whipped around, and she gave him a bewildered look. "Whatever makes you think I'm going to see Myles?"

"Aren't you?" he asked, raising an eyebrow.

"Well," she stuttered, "that's not the point."

Gareth grinned.

"Hmm, I'll tell him hi," she said as she disappeared.

Gareth chuckled. Myles and Cordelia deserved happiness. Wouldn't it be something if they found love after losing their spouses?

He settled into his seat, read Ecclesiastes chapter one, and took some notes before moving on to chapter twelve. All four camera screens went dark. Gareth leaned over to power them back on, but nothing happened. He took a deep breath and tilted his head to the left.

What could have caused the cameras to stop working? The electricity hadn't gone out so that it couldn't be that.

The front door clicked into place. Almost like someone was trying to shut it without being heard. For the first time in years, Gareth reached for his gun.

Gareth rested his hand on the butt of his 9mm, eased out of his chair, and tiptoed around the desk. He hid behind the door but kept his hand on his weapon, ready to pull it if necessary.

He prayed this wasn't something from his past returning to haunt him. Over the years, he had meticulously tied up every loose end, ensuring that nothing lingered before stepping into the role of Evangelist.

But a nagging doubt crept in. Could he have overlooked something critical?

Footsteps echoed in the corridor. For a fleeting moment, someone paused outside his office. Gareth weighed his options. He had no desire to harm anyone, but could he do it if he had to? Before he made a decision, the person moved on, their steps fading down the hall.

Gareth quietly slipped out of his office, his senses tingling with a vibrant energy that surged through him like electricity. He hadn't experienced this feeling in years. He inhaled deeply, savoring the rush.

Just then, his twin brother, Cody, emerged from the adjacent bathroom, a playful, lopsided grin spreading across his face. "Hi, little brother," he chimed, his voice instantly increasing Gareth's tension.

Had Gareth just decided he didn't want to harm anyone? After everything Cody had done over the past few years, Gareth would gladly make an exception for his twin.

Chapter 31

Gareth stiffened. "I could've killed you!" He ran his fingers through his hair. "Why would you do this?"

Cody flashed a grin and shrugged. "I was trying to see how rusty you've gotten. That and to remind myself you got the short end of the stick when it comes to looks."

"This isn't a game." Gareth's eyebrows slanted in disapproval. "There are church members who come in and out of this building all the time! Then our secretary, what would you have done if she were here?"

"Lighten up." Cody waved his hands, palms out. "I made sure your secretary was gone before I killed the feed to the camera system."

Gareth shook his head. "That still doesn't make this okay."

Cody ignored Gareth's reprimand. "Who was the hottie?"

"Excuse me?" Gareth's eyebrows pulled together.

"I saw the woman leaving. And man, she looked happy." Cody made a kissing face. "Does baby brother finally have a girlfriend?"

"Stop that." Gareth narrowed his eyes. "She's not my girlfriend. And I'm only a few seconds younger than you and definitely better looking."

"That's debatable. So, is she single?" His eyes opened wide. "Care to share her number?"

Gareth groaned. "Why are you here, Cody?"

All mischief left Cody's face, and he pulled out a bug detector. "We need to talk. But give me a minute."

Cody walked around the two offices, scanning for listening devices. After he seemed satisfied they could speak privately, he motioned for Gareth to come inside the office.

Gareth poured them each a cup of coffee before settling in at his desk.

A deep frown marred Cody's brow. "Remember Antonio Morales?"

Gareth blew his coffee and took a sip. "Yes, I do. That man has alluded capture for years. I assume he's still trafficking?"

"Yes and no. His youngest daughter, Evangeline, was recently killed by a drunk driver. Saying he's not handling it well is putting it mildly."

"I'm sorry to hear that, but what does that have to do with me?"

"Antonio moved into a huge compound two hours from here a couple of years ago. Before you get onto me for not telling you, I didn't want to get you involved."

"Yet here you are."

"Yes. Here I am." Cody looked out the window, a bleak expression on his face. "I don't really have a choice. Antonio decided to step down from running his organization."

Gareth sat up in his seat. "Does that mean Ricardo is taking over?"

"We could only wish." Cody met Gareth's dark stare. "Ricardo's body washed up on the shores of Orange Beach three weeks ago."

Gareth swallowed. "I take it he didn't drown."

Cody licked his lips. "He was executed."

"Kemena." That's the only person from that family that came to Gareth's mind when he thought of someone committing such a brutal murder.

"Now you see why I'm here?" A set of identical eyes met Gareth's black gaze. "We need your help. You're local with a cover already in place. You can make it work."

"I'm not coming back."

Cody sighed. "I know. I tried to tell them, but they wouldn't listen. So that you know, Vincent's here."

Gareth stood up. "The head of Special Operations is here? I thought the man at the restaurant looked familiar. So he's been watching me?"

"Yes, and he's given me twenty-four hours to get you back on board. I'm only here to warn you that he's coming to see you if you turn me down. I already know the answer is no."

Gareth plopped back down in the chair and rubbed his chin. "Has he been following me around? I thought he wanted to remain anonymous."

Cody shrugged. "Yeah. Some things are more important than remaining completely anonymous."

"Does he happen to be bald?" Gareth took a drink of his coffee.

"He is this week." Cody pointed at a Milky Way on Gareth's desk. "Can I have that? I'm starving."

Gareth tossed the candy bar across the desk to Cody. "So, he's still basically anonymous."

"You know it. He values his privacy. I don't even think his name is Vincent." He tore the wrapper and bit off a huge chunk of the candy bar.

"Wow." Gareth's eyes widened. "I'm curious about his story, but I realize taking down Kemena is the focus."

Cody swallowed the candy bar with a swig of coffee. "Things will get ugly with Kemena in charge. Antonio at least kept things pretty low-key. He paid the immigrants to work and gave them a decent life. But Kemena won't. She's evil, Gareth."

"I can't go back to my old life, Cody. I'm not the same person I was a few years ago. My life belongs to God. He comes first in all things."

"I know. The big wigs were hoping you'd change your mind. We plan on taking Kemena down quickly and need all the help we can get. And you're the best. You know, after me."

"Haha. The answer is still no. I'll keep this situation in my prayers. That's the best I can do."

Chapter 32

Keatyn pulled into the parking lot at Pensacola Water Sports and killed the engine on Dad's truck. She took a deep breath and got out.

The sun beat down, causing dots of sweat to bead across her body. But Keatyn didn't care. As long as the wind carried the aroma of fish sandwiches and sunscreen mixed together, she breathed in a bit of happiness. Her body thrummed with tingles, thinking of doing something outside her comfort zone.

She strolled through the area where locals typically came to relax on the bayside of the ocean. A woman with chocolate hair lay kicked back in a lawn chair. "Sylvia?"

Sylvia raised her hand in greeting. "Well, hello, Keatyn."

Happy, she hadn't accosted a stranger, Keatyn's grin doubled. "Hi. Looks like you had the same idea I did."

Sylvia wagged her head, and a laugh broke from her chest. "I have to take every opportunity to relax that I can."

"Ahh, I get it." Keatyn's expression dawned with understanding. "I see you don't have your twins."

Sylvia massaged the back of her neck. "The boys are with my parents, so I get to read a book and listen to the waves."

A boat motor sprang to life, and Keatyn shielded her eyes as it sped off into deeper water.

For two heartbeats, Keatyn considered abandoning her plan. Then, an idea formed, and she turned to Sylvia, her eyes shining bright as she spoke. "Are you up for an adventure?"

Sylvia leaned on her elbow and met Keatyn's gaze. "An adventure? Sounds intriguing. What did you have in mind?"

Keatyn rocked on her heels. "I came here to go parasailing but am a bit nervous. Wanna ride tandem?"

Sylvia squealed and hopped out of her lawn chair. "That's the best offer I've had in a long time."

Despite the curious stares, Keatyn and Sylvia laughed so hard that they held onto one another as they waded to the shore.

"That was awesome." Keatyn fell onto the sand.

"The best idea ever." Sylvia landed directly to Keatyn's left. She leaned up on her elbow and touched Keatyn's arm. "Thank you for inviting me to do that. It took my mind off things."

Keatyn brushed the sand off her legs. "Hey, you did me a favor going with me. I probably would've chickened out without you."

"We should make this a monthly thing."

"Agreed. I can't wait for the next one. Shake on it?" Keatyn suggested eagerly.

"Absolutely. Same place. Same time. Once a month." Sylvia swayed her neck from side to side and pursed her lips.

Keatyn gurgled with laughter. "Hey, can I ask you something?"

"Sure." Sylvia wiped the moisture off her forehead. "As long as I can ask you something first."

"Ask away."

"You hungry?" Sylvia grinned.

"Famished." Keatyn rose like a wasp had tagged her backside.

Sylvia followed suit and took off across the sand, resting her eyes on Keatyn. "Well, I say we head down the street and split a Shrimp Boat."

"Next to parasailing, I'd say that's the best idea ever." Keatyn rested her hand on her stomach as she paraded across the sand.

Thirty minutes later, an explosion of coconut hit Keatyn's taste buds as she bit into a large piece of shrimp. "I think this idea was better than parasailing. This is soooo good."

Sylvia took a swig of her drink and nodded. "This place has the best shrimp I've ever eaten."

Keatyn craned her neck as a plane flew by. "And just look at that view. I haven't eaten here in ages."

They had chosen to sit on the patio, closer to the water. The patio was a vibrant space, one section with bright blue and orange booths and umbrellas, and the other with tall tables under an overhanging. A playground, places to play games, and a stage where local bands played on weekends completed the outdoor space.

This was the place for locals, especially those with families. The bands were always family-friendly, and the food wasn't too costly.

The kids squealed as they played on the jungle gym in the sand while their parents watched. The dad had a massive smile on his face, even though his hands and shoulders had gotten sunburned. He seemed to be happy just to be there.

And who wouldn't?

Sylvia smiled at the kids before turning back to Keatyn. "Plus there's always a bunch of happy people here."

Keatyn cringed. "Even the sunburned ones."

"They're some of the happiest." Sylvia tucked a stray hair into her ball cap. "I hate to bring it up, but what did you want to ask me earlier?"

"I was thinking about being nosy." Keatyn scooted forward in the booth. "You know about you and Alvin."

Sylvia glanced at her hands and sighed. "That's complicated."

Keatyn swallowed down a bite of hush puppies. "Wouldn't you know I'm super good at complicated."

"Long story short, I like Alvin. I mean, he's gorgeous and so kind." Mist pooled In Sylvia's eyes. "But he's not Lee. I'm sorry if I've hurt him in any way. That's not been my intention."

Keatyn's forehead creased with concern. "Hey. Don't you worry about that. Alvin's a big boy. He cares about you, Sylvia."

"I know that. But I honestly don't think he's in love with me." A worried expression flitted across her face, betraying her inner turmoil. "At least, I hope not. I'm just not ready."

"Only time will tell. I know my brother is a patient man. Have you seen him since he's been home?"

"No, but I've talked to him on the phone." She stared at the sprite rolling around in her glass as she swirled the ice. "He sounds good."

"Yeah, he is. His leg was already on the way to normal when he got home. He's just taking it easy. He's coming to church on Sunday. You should come."

"I'm glad he's doing better. And I'll think about it."

"I hope you do." Keatyn scanned the tables and lowered her voice to a low whisper. "But I have another important question."

Sylvia's brow furrowed, and she leaned in, matching Keatyn's lowered tone. "Go ahead. I'm ready."

Keatyn cracked a grin and raised her voice a little. "Are you going to eat your last piece of coconut shrimp? Cause if you're not, I'll totally help you out with that."

A laugh broke from Sylvia's chest. "It's all yours."

Chapter 33

The sun hung in the sky, casting a warm glow as the temperature flirted with eighty degrees. It was the perfect day for lounging by the shore with Aunt Tanya. The gentle waves lapping at the sand created a soothing soundtrack, inviting them to unwind.

Earlier that morning, Alvin, Myles, and Rodney had set off on their adventure to explore local flea markets, leaving Keatyn in awe of their determination, especially with Alvin navigating on crutches. Their enthusiasm was infectious, and even if it seemed a bit wild, it made them happy, which was what truly mattered.

Seizing the chance to have some quality time together, Aunt Tanya and Keatyn decided to indulge in a much-deserved girls' day. Aunt Tanya unfolded their vibrant beach chairs with a contented smile, preparing their little oasis by the water's edge. The salty breeze tousled Keatyn's hair as she settled into her chair, anticipation bubbling within her for the relaxing day ahead.

"Hello," Keatyn answered her ringing phone as she sprayed sunscreen on her lower legs.

A deep voice answered. "Hello."

Keatyn's heart thumped wildly. "Hi, Gareth."

"I was wondering if I could come for our walk today."

The thumping in her heart doubled if that was even possible. "Um, sure. I'm here with Aunt Tanya, but you can come anytime."

"Perfect. Lily's with me, and I know she'd love to see Tanya."

"Okay. What time will you be here?"

"I can be there in fifteen minutes."

"Sounds good. See you then."

Keatyn glanced at Aunt Tanya. "Gareth and Lily are on their way here."

Aunt Tanya perused Keatyn's flushed face and let out a giggle. "Alrighty."

Keatyn turned on her heel and hightailed it back to the house. "I'll be right back."

"I never would've dreamed you'd have a crush on the preacher." Aunt Tanya mumbled under her breath.

That stopped Keatyn in her tracks. "What did you say?"

Aunt Tanya nodded and smiled before lying back in the chair. "You get on inside. I'll be here listening to the waves."

Keatyn almost tripped over her own feet, trying to rush inside. She poured her makeup case out on the bed. Wait. Who wore makeup on the beach? Only women looking for a man. Right?

It's not like she wanted to impress that man. He's a preacher, and she was not interested in dating him.

Surveying her reflection in the mirror, she added a layer of mascara and pink lip gloss. That would have to be good enough.

When she returned to the beach, an aroma of citrus mixed with wood and a scent Keatyn couldn't place caused her to smile. "Mmm, that citrus smells good, Aunt Tanya."

"That does smell good." The voice that had recently started invading Keatyn's thoughts replied.

Oh no. Raising, Keatyn took off her oversized sunglasses and smiled at Gareth as he strolled through the sand. "Hi."

"Hi." Those dimples. Again.

"Where's Lily?"

"Oh, she's coming. Some seashells got her attention." He nodded behind Keatyn.

She followed his gaze and grinned. Lily had her hands full of shells and her hot pink capris splattered with sand. The look of glee on her face made Keatyn feel some way she couldn't quite describe.

Lily skipped over. "Look what I found." A sweet laugh broke from her chest.

"Those are beautiful." Aunt Tanya heaved herself out of the chair and perused the shells. "What do you say to the two of us looking for more shells while your dad and Keatyn talk?"

"Okay." Lily jumped up and down.

Keatyn pointed at a bag beside her chair. "Lily, there are some nets and a baggie in there you can use."

"Oh, thank you." Lily rummaged through the bag, pulling out the items.

Gareth leaned down and kissed Lily's cheek. "I'll just be over here. Be good for Mrs. Tanya."

"I will."

Gareth and Keatyn walked in silence for a few minutes before they tried to speak at the same time. Keatyn giggled. "You go first."

Gareth scratched his arm before swatting at a bug. "You can go first if you want."

Keatyn stood her ground. "Nope. You go."

"Well, I was just about to bring up the man you seem so interested in."

Heat flushed her cheeks. She guessed Gareth didn't want to waste any time. She looked at the open sea before letting her gaze drift to his. "Is it that obvious?"

He studied her face for a moment before answering. "Who are you referring to?"

She pried her eyes away from his. "Who were you referring to?"

"I asked first." He swallowed loudly.

The heat on her cheeks worked overtime, making her want to pass out. He was talking about the man at the restaurant. Not himself. Now, what should she say?

Hasn't everyone always said honesty is the best policy? Pushing aside her fear, Keatyn rotated her shoulders and looked him square in the face. "I was referring to you."

Surprise etched across Gareth's face.

Great.

He didn't feel the same way.

Before Gareth could say anything, she interrupted him. "Look, Gareth, we both know this won't work. We're too different. So don't feel like you need to respond or tell me about that man following you. It's not my business."

With that, Keatyn turned and rushed into the house.

Gareth shouted something, but Keatyn couldn't understand it. Not that it mattered. She shouldn't have expected anything different.

Chapter 34

Keatyn walked up the sidewalk to attend Sunday service, feeling a bounce in her step. Uncle Rodney smiled as he helped Alvin follow closely behind Keatyn and Myles on his crutches.

As they entered the building, Aunt Tanya greeted them with open arms. "Good morning!" she said, handing Keatyn a bulletin and giving her a kiss on the cheek.

Once they were in the auditorium, everyone exchanged greetings. Keatyn smoothed down the hem of her skirt, remembering the letter she had given Rodney before the service. She pinched the bridge of her nose and closed her eyes for a moment. When she opened them again, she was met with a familiar set of dimples.

"Good morning, Keatyn and family." Gareth's deep voice and the fact that he used her name only caused a brief tickle in her stomach.

"Morning." Keatyn licked her lips and glanced around the building, hoping to see Rebecca.

"Good morning." Several church members greeted the preacher as he made his way down the aisle.

Why did he say Keatyn's name first? Could it be that he's trying to emphasize his lack of interest? If she didn't stop thinking this way, she might as well run out of the building. What she really needed was to regain control of herself. He probably didn't mean anything by it. Or did he?

"Keatyn?" Alvin coughed. "Dad can't stand here all day, you know."

"Oh." Her neck burned like fire. "Sorry." She moved on down the pew, Dad claiming the seat beside her.

Alvin settled in on the other side of Dad. His grin told her he knew something was happening with her and Gareth.

He leaned in and motioned for her to come closer. "Sis. We need to talk later about your feelings."

Keatyn shrank away from Alvin. "You better not say another word."

He put his hand over his mouth and cleared his throat. "I won't. At least not here."

Her eyes shot daggers at Alvin as he pressed his lips together. He looked like he was doing his best not to laugh. "This is not a laughing matter."

"I'm sorry, Sis. I can't help it."

Sylvia chose that moment to walk into the building, with Rhyland and Oakland traipsing in beside her.

Keatyn nodded her head towards the entrance and grinned at Alvin. "Two can play that game."

Alvin turned his head toward the front of the auditorium and blanched. "Okay, I'll hush."

"I figured you'd say that." Keatyn stepped over Dad, and they scooted down to the middle of the pew before waving Sylvia over. "We saved you a seat."

Sylvia tugged her shirt down lower on her hips and waved. "Morning, y'all." She put her hand on Alvin's shoulder. "Hey there, stranger. How are you?"

"I can't complain. How are you?" Rhyland held his arms out to Alvin, and he scooped him up.

One of the elders greeted Sylvia with his hand out. "Welcome. I'm Daniel Bradford, and we're thankful you're here."

Rebecca and Kyle stood beside Daniel. "Hello and welcome," Kyle said.

First Rebecca, then Kyle shook Sylvia's hand. "Good morning. I'm Rebecca, and this is my husband, Kyle."

Sylvia smiled, "I'm Sylvia Mason, and these two are my boys, Rhyland and Oakland."

"Hi there. We're so happy to meet you." Rebecca clapped her hands and asked Sylvia, "Are you okay with them coming to Bible class?"

She ran a finger through her hair. "I'm fine with that. If they'll go."

Gareth and Lily walked up. "Good morning." Gareth shook Sylvia's hand. "We're so thankful you decided to come our way. Hi, boys. I'm Gareth, and this is my daughter, Lily."

"Good morning." Sylvia glanced at Keatyn. "Keatyn invited me."

After they finished introductions, Gareth's eyes landed on Keatyn, and she gasped, followed by a choke.

Alvin handed her a cough drop. "Here you go, Sis." He covered his mouth with the back of his hand, and Keatyn figured he was on the verge of losing it. It's a good thing service was about to start.

Lily waved at the boys, and Oakland grinned. "Is Lily in class?"

Rebecca replied, "Yes, she is in our class."

"I'll go!" Rhyland announced.

"Me too!" Oakland agreed.

Sylvia watched as her boys followed Rebecca and Lily out of the auditorium. "Hmm. That went better than I anticipated."

"I'm glad," Keatyn grinned before focusing on the Bible class lesson.

Chapter 35

Keatyn broke out in a cold sweat and nearly ran out of the church building again, just as she had several months ago. Gareth had delivered a sermon from the book of Ecclesiastes that captivated her. It was both accurate and relevant to people today. Just because there would never be anything romantic between them didn't mean she couldn't appreciate his sermons. After all, he was a powerful speaker.

After the invitation song, Uncle Rodney went down the aisle, and Keatyn's chest rose and fell with rapid breaths. Dad took Keatyn's hand and engulfed it in his. The pure love written in his eyes calmed her breathing. He was proud of her. The tension in her shoulders seemed to ease as her body relaxed. She laid her head on his shoulder, and he put his arm around her.

Rodney stopped at the podium and pulled the piece of paper Keatyn had given him out of his pocket. He leaned down and spoke into the microphone. "Keatyn Griffin asked me to read this letter to the congregation this morning."

"For the past ten years, I haven't lived up to the Christian values my parents instilled in me. I've made choices that I regret, allowing my grief to turn into anger with Satan's influence. I want to change. I want to be a woman my mother would have been proud to call her daughter and make my father proud. Most importantly, I want to honor God. My life belongs to Christ, and I sincerely hope you can forgive me for the shame I have brought the church over the years."

As Rodney prayed on Keatyn's behalf, a weight lifted from her heart with each word. He then reminded everyone to stay for a potluck luncheon before ending the service with a closing prayer.

Sylvia's eyes brimmed with tears as she hugged Keatyn. "Wow, that took a lot of courage. I'm happy for you."

After hugging a long line of people, they headed downstairs for their potluck luncheon. The room hadn't changed over the years. The ample space held around twenty round tables spread about the area. It had been decorated with a bee theme. Posters and decorations about "Beeing Kind" and "Beeing Happy" lined the walls. And each table had a light-yellow plastic tablecloth with various bee centerpieces.

Memories of running around those tables as a child flooded Keatyn's mind. She remembered Mama telling her to slow down and the hugs and kisses she received whenever she fell and scraped her knee.

These were good memories that Keatyn chose to cherish. She knew Mama was now in paradise and that she would see her again one day. Mama would want her to be happy, so the bee theme felt just right.

Keatyn shared a bug-eyed grin with Alvin when Cordelia told Dad she would make his plate. She had to excuse herself from the table when Cordelia pranced up with a container filled with enough food for three people.

All kinds of sugary delights filled the dessert table. Keatyn tapped her chin as her eyes roamed the table.

"I recommend the chocolate cupcake," Gareth whispered next to her, glancing around the room as if he were about to reveal a great secret. "Nobody realizes how good they are, and I don't share that information with many people."

"Well, how can I say no to that?" Keatyn's eyes sparkled as she scooped up a cupcake and turned to leave.

He gently touched her forearm, sending a warm thrill through her. "Can we talk?"

"Sure," she replied, glancing at the cupcake. "What's on your mind?"

Gareth removed his hand from her arm and stuck it in his pocket. "You left before I could answer you the other day."

Keatyn surveyed the room. Most of the adults looked in their direction. She scratched the place he'd touched with a shaky hand. "I know I was out of line, and I'm sorry about that."

"You were not out of line." Gareth glanced around the room. At least ten more people fixed their eyes on him and Keatyn. "I'm the one who owes you an apology. I should've admitted my feelings long before now."

"Feelings?" Her breath hitched in her throat.

"I would like to spend time with you and get to know you better, Keatyn. However, you need to understand that I only date with long-term intentions."

In an instant, Keatyn's mouth dropped open in surprise, and a flush of red colored her tan skin. "I'd like that," she replied.

Long-term intentions? A desire to twirl around and jump in the air hit Keatyn hard. But people would wonder about her sanity.

A smile jotted across Gareth's lips. "Is there room for me at your table?"

Dad and Cordelia had already vacated their seats and moved over with Aunt Tanya. That left Alvin and Sylvia alone. Keatyn would have to ask Alvin about how that went later. But for now, all she could do was smile. "Yes, of course. Please join us."

He entwined his hand with hers as they meandered to the table.

Lily chose that moment to cackle out at something, and a smile touched Keatyn's lips. She was home. Finally.

Chapter 36

Late fall on Pensacola Beach had to be one of the best times of the year, in Keatyn's opinion. It was warm, but not too warm. And the sky held a beauty that couldn't be passed.

Who was she kidding? She loved all times of the year on Pensacola Beach. And after her meeting with Jean Cordell, it would again be her permanent residence. She'd officially accepted the VP position in the Gulf States and would dive back into work full-time in a few days.

She would be the VP, but she had an idea of opening a restaurant on a boat. She wasn't sure when or even if that would happen, but she hoped her dream would one day come to fruition.

While in Seattle the last time, Keatyn had searched out Peter and Lucy. She'd swallowed her pride and asked for their forgiveness. They'd both been shocked but had granted her request. Maybe she and Lucy would never be close friends, but at least Keatyn had been able to make amends.

Excitement thrummed through her body with the thought of living on Pensacola Beach. With Gareth and Lily. She knew in her heart that's where she belonged.

A Preacher's wife. At least she hoped and prayed Gareth would one day ask her to marry him. A year ago, she would've fought someone if they'd told her she'd be in love with a preacher. But now. Now, she couldn't imagine her life taking any other path.

The door to her convertible Infiniti snapped shut behind her, and she grabbed her beach bag. She needed some time alone to pray and ponder what was next. So she'd rented a boat, and her insides thrummed with nervous energy.

She desperately wanted to do what was right, and for that, she needed God's help. She'd pray for His will to be done and leave her life in His capable hands.

After paying and loading, she boarded the boat and sped deep into Pensacola Bay.

The boat skimmed over the water, beating against the waves as Keatyn cruised the waters of Pensacola Bay.

She admired the houses along the shore and waved at other boaters as they passed by. She took a sip of her water and killed the boat's engine, deciding to simply float around and relax for a while.

Being alone with her thoughts had been the perfect medicine. She never would've dreamed she'd spend time alone in prayer like she had today. She couldn't have asked for a more perfect day.

After a couple of hours, she headed back to the docks. Her hair beat against her face as the wind fought with her ballcap. A few minutes later, she eased the boat into the docking station.

She grabbed her beach bag and made her way down the dock. A woman's shrill laughter caught Keatyn's attention, and she glanced in the direction it came from.

The woman draped herself onto a man who had his back to Keatyn. Her lips trailed his ear, and Keatyn threw up a little bit in her mouth.

Embarrassed for witnessing their public display of affection, she started to walk away. The man turned.

Keatyn stopped dead in her tracks. "Gareth?" A little gasp escaped her lips.

Black eyes full of disdain met her astonished expression.

Her spine jerked into motion, and she slowly backed away before her mind forced her legs to break into a run.

"Hey, wait!" Came from the boat.

From Gareth.

Her mind trembled, and she ignored his pleas for her to stop. Could he be leading a double life? Had he been playing Keatyn this whole time?

Once in the parking lot, she fumbled with her keys and jerked the car door open. What a fool she'd been. But never again.

Never.

A horn blaring followed by screeching tires caught Keatyn's attention. Her stomach dropped when a white van skidded right in her direction.

Gareth pulled into the parking lot just as Keatyn sped towards the exit. He'd planned to surprise her with flowers after she got off the boat. Flowers and a confession.

It was time to come clean. He had to fill Keatyn in on his history. It's not like he'd broken any laws or anything. It was just a history he didn't want to share with everyone. That had been his plan. To tell her everything.

Sometimes, plans didn't work out so well. What could have happened to cause her to be upset?

Cody barreled down the dock and met Gareth's gaze. He shook his head and pointed at Keatyn's car as it screeched out of the parking lot.

Gareth didn't waste another moment. He jammed the Ford F-150 into gear, and the engine sprang to life. His tires left black marks as he pulled out of the parking lot.

Only a few cars separated them, so he should be able to catch her. She must've met Cody. But what would've made her react the way she did? He groaned when he had to stop for a few people walking across the street. His eyes followed a helicopter flying by as he waited on the pedestrians. As soon as the people got across the road, he scanned the road ahead for Keatyn. Just as she got knocked into the bridge railing by a white van involved in a three-car pile-up.

Chapter 37

The following morning, Alvin told Gareth that Keatyn was resting and wasn't up to visitors. He suggested trying back the next day.

Gareth said a prayer of thanks that Keatyn and the rest of the people involved hadn't gotten severely hurt. Keatyn's sprained wrist would heal over time.

He called Cody, and they agreed to meet that evening for dinner at Los Sayaro's in Mary Esther. He had to figure out what had happened at the docks.

At the restaurant, Gareth hit Cody with a fierce gaze after settling into a secluded booth. "Tell me what happened."

Cody crossed his legs. "First of all, I'm thankful your not-girlfriend is all right."

Gareth took a deep breath. He couldn't allow his emotions to get the better of him. He had an example to set for his brother, after all. "I appreciate that.

Maybe she and I have become more than friends. At least we had. Before whatever stunt you pulled."

Cody twirled his hair. It had grown out and was a bit longer than Gareth's. "She saw what appeared to be a woman in an embrace with me."

Gareth bunched his hands into fists. "What?"

"Hold on." Cody put his palms up. "It's not like that."

"Then explain what it is like." Gareth's eyes shot daggers. "Now."

Cody scanned the restaurant before he spoke in a lowered voice. "It was Kemena Morales. Threatening me."

Gareth's tone matched Cody's. "Kemena?"

"Yes. She embraced me and whispered in my ear that a bomb was under the dock. To the passerby, it would've looked like a couple's embrace."

Gareth closed his eyes and ran a hand through his hair. "I'm glad no one was hurt. Or was there?"

"No. The bomb squad came dressed like tourists and shut it down." He leaned across the table. "We were also able to apprehend Kemena."

Condensation dripped down Gareth's glass of ice water. He ran his finger around the rim, fighting memories from another life away. "So there was a bomb?"

"Yes. I had no doubt. She told me if anyone made a move on her, the bomb would be detonated, killing everyone on the dock, including herself."

"I do not miss this life. And I don't want to be involved in any of it. More importantly, I don't want innocent people to lose their lives."

Cody's eyes lit up with hope. "Does that mean what I think it does?"

Gareth twiddled with a toothpick while shaking his head. "I stand by my answer from before."

"That's what I thought you'd say. That means someone else will need to be stationed in this area. The rest of the Morales family need to be taken down." A mischievous grin flashed across Cody's face. "Wouldn't you just love having me closer?"

Gareth chuckled. "The jury's still out. But I do need a favor."

"Anything." Cody sat up straighter in his seat.

"Come with me to meet Keatyn."

Chapter 38

The day Keatyn graduated from college had been both good and bad. Good because she'd made it through three of the worst years of her life. Bad because of the way she'd acted toward her family.

She could still remember the hatred seeping like rot through her bones. She never wanted to feel that way again. That meant she had to let go of whatever Gareth had done and move forward. If not, she had a sinking feeling that bitterness would overtake her. Even though she knew she'd let it go, she could not bring herself to face him. Yet.

Aunt Tanya had taken it upon herself to be Keatyn's nurse. She hadn't left Keatyn's side and was curled up in the chair beside the bed, going back and forth between reading a book and talking.

Keatyn lay as perfectly still in bed as possible. Right now, she'd do anything to have a moment's peace to think through her situation. She needed a clear head, but that wouldn't happen soon with Aunt Tanya talking a mile a minute.

A few church members, including the elders, had been in and out of the house over the past day and a half. They meant well, and it felt good to know people cared. Thankfully, Aunt Tanya kept most of them in the living room. Keatyn would rather eat a bug than see many people right now.

The accident could've been so much worse. What if someone had been walking on the bridge? She shuddered with the thought.

The doorbell rang again. Probably another church member checking on her. At least, that's what she thought until a new voice rang through the bedroom door.

Could that be Lucy Parnell?

A few seconds passed before Dad poked his head inside the room. "Are you up for a visit from your friend Lucy?"

Keatyn raised on an elbow and pulled the cover over her side. Even though Lucy had forgiven her, Keatyn still had a nervous anticipation swirling inside her stomach. "Of course, I am."

Lucy strode inside the room, her eyes full of unshed tears. "I heard about your wreck."

A smile whisked across Keatyn's face, and she held her hand out. "I'm so glad you came. Who told you I had a wreck?"

Lucy rubbed her hands together, and her voice seemed to have a nervous edge to it. "Peter's mom heard about it."

Keatyn would do anything to put Lucy's mind at ease. She had a lot of making up to do. "Oh, that makes sense. You're letting your hair grow out. I love it."

Light crimson stained Lucy's cheeks, and she swallowed, her throat constricting. It dawned on Keatyn that she'd never complimented Lucy before. She may need to ask Aunt Tanya to get another chair so Lucy didn't hit the ground.

Lucy took Keatyn's outstretched hand. Her free hand went to her curls, pulling a few behind her ear. "Thanks, Keat. I was worried about you."

"I'm doing really good." A gentle puff of a laugh left her. "You know, other than getting knocked into bridges."

Lucy's laughter rang out, signaling the fading tension. Her shoulders dropped in a visible sign of relaxation, bringing a wave of relief to Keatyn.

Aunt Tanya must've read Keatyn's mind. She lifted herself out of the chair and patted Keatyn's hand. "I'll just be in the living room if you need me."

Keatyn hugged Aunt Tanya's hand to her chest and smiled. "Thank you, Aunt Tanya."

Aunt Tanya beamed as she made her way out of the room.

Keatyn and Lucy spent the next hour catching up and rebuilding their friendship. Another answered prayer.

Chapter 39

The brand-new iPhone sparkled in Keatyn's hand as she left the cell phone store. Almost a week had passed since her accident, and she felt much better.

At least her body did. Her heart still ached. She couldn't understand how Gareth had done whatever he'd done. She'd thought he meant forever. Maybe she'd been wrong. The pain was a constant companion, a heavy weight she couldn't shake off.

She pictured Gareth as he'd appeared on the docks. He'd looked like Gareth, but not exactly. He had been the same but also different. Not that it mattered. Anyone could change their appearance to match the occasion. It happened all the time.

Even though he'd tried to see her multiple times since the accident, she'd turned him away. Dad and Alvin had shared their unwanted opinions numerous times, but she'd stuck to her guns. She needed time and space. And that's what she meant to have.

Against her better judgment, she finally agreed to meet Gareth on the Pensacola Pier. The thought of seeing him today increased her breathing and heart rate. She'd missed church Sunday after her accident but would see him Wednesday, so it was better to get it over with privately. The anticipation was almost unbearable.

She had some house hunting to do this afternoon. Dad and Cordelia had asked the family to meet, and Keatyn suspected they had a special announcement to make. So, she'd need to find another place to live before Dad and Cordelia married. There was no way she'd live with Dad and a new wife. Not even one as nice as Cordelia.

She stepped down the pier, and her stomach churned. Gareth leaned against the rail with his back to her. She took a moment to study his profile before he turned in her direction.

Keatyn stopped a few feet away from him, thankful the warm wind hit her cheeks, hiding the fact that her face had blood-red splotches all over it.

The corners of his mouth lifted into a grin. "I'm so glad you're okay. We missed you at service yesterday."

Keatyn's eyes darted away from his gaze. "Thank you. What is it you wanted to talk to me about?"

He motioned down the pier. "First, I want to introduce you to my brother."

Blowing out a breath, she gazed at him. "Your brother?"

A voice sounded behind her. "Keatyn?"

Turning, she met a pair of jet-black eyes. She jerked her head around and met another set of jet-black eyes. The color drained from her face. "What's going on?"

"Keatyn, this is my twin, Cody." The grin Gareth displayed earlier transformed into a full-fledged, ear-splitting smile. "Cody, this is Keatyn."

Rubbing her temples, she met Cody's eyes. The difference jumped out plain as day. The main one was how Cody's eyes seemed hard while Gareth's displayed kindness.

Keatyn wrapped her hand around her throat. "It was you and your wife on the pier?"

Cody shrugged, "You have part of it right."

Keatyn bunched her eyebrows together. "Hopefully, the part where it was you."

He seemed to scan the area before he answered. "Yes, it was me on the boat."

This brother was a little odd. Thankfully, she'd met Gareth first, or she might have been running in another direction. "And your girlfriend?"

"Not exactly."

She lowered her voice, but her demeanor took on that of a boss. She took a step closer to Cody. "Then you better explain what you mean."

"Let's just say the woman is someone I have some issues with."

"Honestly, it's none of my business." Biting her lip, Keatyn glanced at the ground. "Gareth, I owe you an apology."

He gripped her hand in his. "No, you don't. Anyone would've thought the same thing. I'd never told you I have a twin."

"That is true." She shifted her feet as she met Gareth's gaze. "Is this why the man has been following you?"

Cody nodded. "I'm sorry if I've caused problems."

"No apology necessary."

Gareth's shoulders relaxed. "I'd like to move on from here. That is if you're still interested in a relationship with me?"

Sagging against the rail, Keatyn swallowed down the emotion that threatened to spill over. "More than you know."

Cody clapped his hands together. "Now that that's settled, I'm heading out. I have things to take care of. Keatyn, it was nice officially meeting you. I hope we can start fresh." His words were polite, but Keatyn couldn't shake the feeling that there was more to his story.

"You, too." She squeezed Gareth's hands as Cody disappeared down the pier. "Dad and Cordelia are about to announce they're engaged. Wanna come to the party?"

Gareth's eyes popped, and he grasped her hand tighter. "Engaged? How did I miss that?"

She swallowed, her head spinning with how things had changed. One minute, she'd determined to be alone forever. The next minute, she had a relationship with Gareth on her mind. "They haven't said anything yet. But I've been watching them for the past few months. I knew it would happen sooner or later."

"Then what are we waiting for? Let's go to a party."

Chapter 40

Keatyn crunched an apple from the kitchen bar, captivated by birds soaring above the shimmering ocean, their wings outstretched as they dipped and glided effortlessly. With each graceful plunge, they splashed into the crystal-clear waves, sending droplets glimmering like diamonds into the air. No matter how often she witnessed this spectacle, it filled her with a sense of wonder.

"I see you have a smile from ear to ear this morning." Alvin limped into the kitchen. "Things must still be going well with you and preacher man."

The doctor said Alvin's limp may or may not heal. Only time will tell. Alvin said he didn't care either way. He could've lost his life, so having a limp wasn't a problem. God had seen him and his entire unit through their mission, so Alvin wouldn't dream of complaining.

"Yes, if you must know, *Gareth* and I couldn't be better." Keatyn rolled her eyes and play-punched Alvin in the shoulder.

Things had gone more than well over the past few months. She'd even gotten to know his twin, Cody, better. He was staying somewhere outside of Milton to be close to whatever he was working on. She gathered he held a job in law enforcement, but that's all she cared to know.

Warmth spread up her arms and into her heart, thinking of Gareth.

"Good to hear." He pooched out his bottom lip. "Would you pretty please take me out for a cup of coffee?"

She raised her eyebrow. "I can make you a better cup of coffee here than you can get in town, little brother."

His shoulders slumped like he had just been dealt a blow. "I know, but I was hoping we'd run into a certain somebody."

"Alrighty then." He must have Sylvia on the brain. She hated to break it to him, but he needed to let Sylvia have her space. Instead of telling him what she thought, she grabbed the keys and stared at him while she tapped her foot. "Let's go before I change my mind."

An hour later, Keatyn pulled back down the drive to the cottage, Alvin and her holding a cup of expensive coffee.

A giant pink bow hung from the front door. She glanced at Alvin with a question in her eyes. "Somebody having a girl I don't know about?"

He averted his gaze before jumping out. "Let's go in and see."

Keatyn and Alvin stepped over the doorway, and Keatyn took in the room. Nothing seemed to be out of place. "What's going on? Why is there a bow on the door?"

A group of people filed out of the back of the house, singing the Happy Birthday song to Keatyn.

She put her hands on her hip. "Oh, I get it. You didn't want this cup of coffee, did you?"

Alvin shrugged. "Not really. It is a good cup of coffee, though."

When she noticed Sylvia in the group, she laughed. "And I take it you didn't really want to go to town to run into Sylvia. You tricked me."

Her laugh got louder when Alvin's face turned red.

His blush deepened after Sylvia giggled. "I never said a name."

Dad took Keatyn's hands in his and kissed them both. "Do you like your birthday present?"

Keatyn grinned, relishing in the sense of peace that had settled in her heart since she'd let go of the bitterness she'd carried for so long. "I don't need anything, Dad. I'm happy to be here with family and friends."

His eyes held a twinkle like he had years before. "Regardless, I can't let this milestone birthday pass without giving you the present I've worked on for almost ten years."

Rebecca laughed, and little Bliss cooed and laughed along with her. "Oh, you're gonna want this present, believe me."

Keatyn had no idea what they were referring to, but she was curious. "What is it?"

Dad gestured around the cottage with his hand. "This. Didn't you see the bow on the door?"

"This?" She rocketed across the space and threw her arms around his neck. "Oh no, you can't give me your home."

Dad took her arms and stared into her eyes. "Baby girl, I've done all this for you. Alvin and I did this together. All for you."

Cordelia placed her arms around Keatyn's neck. "Your dad will soon have a new home. With me, and I think he'll love it."

"Oh, I know he will, Cordelia. It's just that I never anticipated anything like this." She got out between sobs.

Gareth pushed a cart with a giant cake shaped like a boat to Keatyn. She giggled when she saw it. He nodded at Tanya. "Your Aunt Tanya made this for you. Isn't it awesome?"

"It's the most beautiful cake I've ever seen." Keatyn crossed the room and hugged Aunt Tanya. "Thank you, Aunt Tanya."

"You're welcome, my dear." She wiped a few tears away. "Our lives are finally whole again now that you're home."

Gareth cleared his throat. "Keatyn, there's something on the cake. Can you come over here, please?"

Beside him, Lily jumped up and down, seemingly unable to contain her excitement. Keatyn arched a questioning eyebrow in his direction. "Sure."

A gleam hit her in the eye when she approached the cake. Her stomach quivered, and she swallowed down a gulp of air.

This can't be happening. She must be dreaming.

Gareth pulled the gleaming object off the cake and fell on one knee.

Her heart hitched, and she wavered. Dad grabbed her arms, or she may have hit the ground.

"Keatyn Rae Griffin, my life changed the very day we met. I had no doubt you'd make my life better. I didn't know how much better it would be with you in it. I love you."

Gareth glanced down at Lily, and she grasped Keatyn's hand. "And I wuv you!"

Gareth beamed at Keatyn. "Will you do me the honor of becoming my wife?"

"Nothing would make me happier than marrying you, Gareth. I love you." She pulled Lily to her side. "And I love you, my sweet girl."

Epilogue

Six months later

Keatyn held onto Dad's arm for dear life. He leaned down and kissed the top of her head. "You ready, my dear?"

Her eyes gleamed as she watched the bridal party getting ready to walk down the aisle. The bridesmaid's dresses sparkled in the moonlight. They were full of sparkly pink and glitter and fell just below the knee with the sleeves ending above the elbow.

They decided to have their wedding on the beach in what would soon be their backyard. White chairs lined the aisle, with pink and purple flowers draped across the backs. Rodney stood by Gareth under a simple white arch, ready to perform the nuptials.

Sylvia and Alvin started down the aisle first, followed by Rebecca and Kyle. Lily came next in her white gown. She had asked if she could wear white like Keatyn, and Keatyn had readily agreed. They planned to start proceedings for Keatyn to adopt Lily after they got settled, so she was thrilled that Lily looked up to her already.

It had blown Keatyn's mind when Gareth admitted he'd been in the CIA before he left to become a preacher. At least she wouldn't have to worry about protection. Not with that hunk of a man by her side.

A grin tugged at Keatyn's lips as she gently traced the intricate lace patterns of mama's wedding gown, a cherished relic from the eighties. Unaltered and preserved, the dress held a nostalgic charm that resonated with her. To Keatyn, it felt like a warm embrace from Mama, reminding her of the love their family had shared. The graceful long sleeves and cascading hemline made her feel regal and connected to Mama, while the pearls shimmered softly throughout the gown.

Thinking of the sparkly white flip-flops she wore under the dress caused a giggle to escape. She met Dad's eyes. "I'm more than ready, Dad."

"I love you, Keatyn."

"And I love you."

Finally, it was Keatyn's turn. She floated down the aisle with her light eyes locked on a set of darker ones. Both sets of eyes were full of misty tears. And love.

Keatyn barely heard anything Uncle Rodney said. Except when he asked if she would take Gareth to be her husband.

"Yes, forever." She whispered.

The ceremony passed in a blur until Uncle Rodney's lips lifted as he met Gareth's eyes. "You may kiss your bride."

That all-so-familiar heat inched up her arms as her husband kissed her for the first time as his wife.

After the ceremony, Keatyn stood in awe at how her life had changed. What a journey she'd been on. It hadn't been an easy one, that's for sure. But it was worth it.

Her heart burst with love. For her family. For her new husband. Her new daughter.

But most of all, her heart was full of love and thanksgiving to God for His love and care. He never gave up on her, even when she'd given up on herself.

Keatyn planned to live her new life to the fullest. Looking to God first for all things. In His service.

Gareth grabbed her hand. "Hello there, Mrs. Davenport.

The sound of her new name riddled Keatyn's skin with goosebumps. "Hello there, Mr. Davenport."

He brushed his lips across her brow. "You ready to start our forever?"

"Already started." She smiled a toothy grin and laid her head on his shoulder, relishing the moment and holding it in her heart.

Thank you for taking the time to read **_Keatyn's Journey_**. If you found it enjoyable, I would be grateful if you could leave a review. Your feedback truly makes a difference!

acknowledgements

When I started this novel, I had the idea to write a few standalone stories about our journeys in life. I wanted to focus on journeys leading us to God, including real-life struggles and examples.

I quickly felt a strong connection as I continued writing and forming these characters in my mind and on paper. Maybe it's because my characters mean something to me. Each journey novel will have a main character in memory of or in honor of someone I love or have a connection to. Yes, I want to be emotional as I write!

The first novel is a work of love written in memory of Keatyn Snead. I can't describe my gratitude for Keatyn's mother, Tania. I'm so humbled she shared her precious daughter's name with me. I named Keatyn's brother Alvin after my brother, whom we lost when I was twelve. So, I think it's fitting that I felt such love for these siblings.

With that being said, I have started on Sylvia's Journey and, Lord willing, plan to continue with many journeys after hers.

I couldn't have picked a better person to be on the first cover of my Journey Series. Samantha - your beauty shines! My photographer, Shelby, captured Samantha's inner and outer beauty in such a fantastic way! I'm so happy we worked together on this!

Thank you to my sister-in-law, Brandie Hudson, for reading and giving me feedback.

I thank my ARC readers from the bottom of my heart! The feedback and encouragement I've received have been so uplifting!

I love and appreciate my husband, Mark, so much for sharing his sermons! He made this novel even more special to me! Sharing the word of God is my end goal, and I love that my hubby is here to help guide me along the way.

Dear readers, I pray you'll continue this journey with me and all our characters along the way.

XOXO

about the author

Leah Brewer is a multi-genre author who focuses on writing clean books that anyone can read. She was born and raised in Des Arc, Arkansas, before moving to Northeast Arkansas when her children were young.

She spends her spare time with her husband, Mark, their grown children, and granddaughter, Charlotte. If she's not on a beach, she's dreaming about when she can be!

Made in the USA
Columbia, SC
02 December 2024